I0600002

POUND FOR POUND

S Lynn C

Golden Light Publishing House

Book Cover by Vikki

Formatting and Developmental Editing by: B Wills

ISBN: 979-8-9928401-4-8

PLAYLIST

Ch 44 Starlight – Starset

Trigger Warnings

Alcohol Consumption
Attempted Crimes
Kidnapping
Offensive Language
Physical Abuse
Sexual Abuse
Sexually Explicit Scenes
Violence

CONTENTS

Chapter 1

Lisey

"If you keep hitting that refresh button, you're going to break it," Mom said, laughing gently behind me. "Then you'll never know."

I hit the refresh button for the hundredth time, anxiously waiting for the email that could change my entire life.

Anxiety blossomed in my chest.

Her hands settled gently on my shoulders.

I glanced at the time.

Half past three.

The deadline was set for fifteen minutes prior.

I slumped in my chair, leaning my head back. Her gorgeous model face peered down at me, her eyes glistening with silent sympathy, making my chest feel heavy.

"I probably didn't get it," I said quietly.

"If you didn't, that's okay. You are a talented young woman and can do anything you put your mind to. If you wanted, you know that Hiram would be thrilled to have you join us at the agency."

I sighed.

Hiram had been trying to get me to join that agency since I was fourteen years old. Here we were, ten years later, and he was still desperate to keep his highest-rated model's legacy alive through me.

I leaned forward again and hit the refresh button. The inbox regenerated and a new email appeared. My heart began to pound in my chest with anticipation.

"It's here."

"Well, go on. Open it," she encouraged.

I clicked on the email.

"Dear Ellisia, we are pleased to welcome you as the lead screenwriter for the upcoming film Pound for Pound. Details will be emailed to you within the coming days. We are pleased to have you on board."

"I got the job!" I jumped up from my chair and hugged her.

"I'm so proud of you."

My heart felt as light as air. I had been working so hard for this very moment. For years, I was the knock-down, drag-out girl, building sets, dealing with arrogant actors and directors. The worst being Kurbrick. Then the opportunity for me to take on screenwriting came.

It had been a long time coming, many late nights and hard work, but it finally paid off.

I could scream.

I practically leapt away from her, excitement bubbling through me.

"I have to call Gerry." I grabbed my phone and stepped out onto the patio.

The phone rang several times.

"Yes." Her tone was clipped.

"I got it!"

"You got it?"

"I'm heading Pound for Pound."

"I told you that you were going to make it out there, kid."

"It's all thanks to you, had you not sent my resume in."

"You earned it. You're my shining star. You deserve this."

My excitement faded as I realized how much work I was leaving behind while I traveled with the movie.

"Who's going to pick up what I leave behind? I'll be gone for months."

"Don't worry about it. I'll divide it between the others. They won't mind." I could hear typing in the background. That woman lived on her computer.

"Are you sure? I could always work on the road."

"Absolutely not, you need to get out there and show them who Ellisia Hammond is." I pulled the phone away from my face as I squealed. I couldn't believe this was happening.

"Thank you, Gerry."

"Go get them, Lisey."

We hung up the phone, and I was startled by the sound of the popping cork of a champagne bottle. Turning, I saw my mother standing with an open bottle of bubbly and two champagne glasses.

"A toast to my brilliant daughter." I sauntered over and took one of the glasses from her. The crystal clinked with a heavenly sound and then I sipped it slowly, feeling the bubbles as they tickled my tongue before traveling down my throat.

"Do you know who they cast for the lead?" Mom asked.

"I have heard rumors, but as far as I know nothing was set in stone yet."

"It will probably be someone big."

"Or someone new."

"Think about it, Lisey. The people you'll meet. The places you'll go. This is the opportunity of a lifetime." Her words pounded in my ears.

For years, I tried to escape her shadow.

My mother was the Elenor Fitz, discovered in the nineties by Hiram at the age of eighteen. She was working in a diner, and he said she had the look, and she still does to this day. Even at the age of forty-five, she doesn't look a day over twenty-five. She still models in London, Paris, and Milan, twice for fashion week.

Everyone always fawned over me, telling me that I would follow in her footsteps as her mirrored image. All of her grace, demeanor and looks were passed to me.

Basically, a clone.

Most people were surprised to find out I was her daughter and not her sister. "What are you thinking about?" I looked up at her, her eyes holding the question as I raised the glass to my lips once more.

"Nothing. I just can't wait to start working on this movie." Her smile beamed as she raised her glass to me once more and took a sip. It was then that the moment was broken by the sound of my phone.

I pulled it from my pocket.

"Daddy's calling." My mother rolled her eyes and walked back into the house with the bottle of champagne. Their marriage was short lived, and their civility was barely tolerable of each other. I answered the call and put the phone to my ear.

"Hi, Dad, it's late, is everything okay?"

"It's only one in the morning here in London." His British accent was thick on the phone. "I set a reminder in my calendar. Today's the big day isn't it?"

"Yes it is."

"Well?" A smile spread across my face.

"I got the job!"

"That's absolutely brilliant my love. Well done."

"Thank you."

"Do you know where the movie is set to film?"

"Not yet, but I know they asked that I had a passport available, so I'm hoping somewhere out of the country."

"What's the film called again?"

"Pound for Pound."

"What's it about? It sounds like a dirty film."

"It's not, Dad. It's like Rocky completely un-hinged."

"Sounds like it's going to be quite the show." His response lacked enthusiasm.

I could feel the tug in my chest like I had many times with him.

My good news never quite seemed good enough, no matter how hard he tried to sound happy.

"I'm really excited." I brushed it off, as I often did.

"As you should be. I'm incredibly proud of you."

If only I could believe that.

"I'm hoping that maybe we will film somewhere near you so that maybe we can meet up."

"I would love that." He was distracted, no doubt checking his emails while we talked.

We grew silent, not abnormal for us we usually had little to talk about.

"Well, my darling, I have to go, business meetings and such in the morning."

"Alright, I'll talk to you soon."

"That you shall."

"I love you."

The call ended and I put my phone down on the table, throwing back the rest of the champagne as the door opened and my mother reappeared from the house.

"How's your father?" she asked.

"Delighted."

"The wife?" Her scorn evident in her words.

"I didn't ask." I twisted the empty glass in my hand, letting the sun catch the crystal and scatter rainbows across the wall.

The silence that followed was so thick, the birds didn't dare sing.

"More champagne?" Mom asked, breaking the tension.

"Yes, please." I held my glass out, and she tipped the bottle until it ran dry, gracing the lip.

"Whoops, looks like we need another bottle," she laughed. I laughed too, then slowly brought the glass to my lips.

CHAPTER 2

Quinn

M y head was pounding, and the persistent banging at the hotel door wasn't helping at all. I went to move my arm but realized it was held down by a weight. Turning my head, there was the unmistakable flame-red hair of the stunning young woman I had brought back from the show. The knocking continued.

"Alright. For fuck's sake!" I groaned as I wrenched my arm from under her and twisted to get up, almost colliding with the brunette that was draped over my other arm. They both grumbled as I got up.

Striding to the door, I ripped it open. The scent of liquor was heavy in the draft. My manager stood prepared to knock once more.

Upon glancing at me, he shielded his face.

"For fuck's sake, Quinn, put some pants on." A small smile pulled at the corner of my lips as I stood there in the doorway in the brisk nude. I leaned against the door frame.

"What is it, Roddy?" He locked eyes with me, his irritation evident as he held up a piece of paper.

"You got the gig." I stood straight and took the paper from him. It was a printed email from Whiplash Productions.

"I got the role?" The headache that lingered immediately took a back seat.

"Yeah, you did." His disgust loud in his tone.

"What about the tour?"

"You only have two more shows. Should be over by the time you are set to leave."

"We cancel."

"The venue has already paid."

"Then we pay them back, hand out refunds." Roddy grumbled under his breath.

"We will cross that bridge when we get to it." Another door down the hall opened and I peered up to see who it was. Barry stepped out of his room, took one look at me, and immediately covered his eyes.

"Dude, come on, it's too early for all that."

"It's four in the afternoon," Roddy scoffed, palming his face.

"Whatever," Barry said.

"I got the role, Bar." He walked over and took the paper from my hand. Barry and I had been friends since we were kids, we started Nitrous Ruin together, no one could out shred him on a bass, or write songs like him.

"This is great, bro!" He held the paper out to Roddy and then punched me in the arm. Roddy took the paper.

"I'll let you two do whatever it is you are going to do. Just don't forget we have a rehearsal in the morning. Try to be on time." His voice was exhausted; poor guy had been being run ragged since day one. We definitely weren't easy on him.

"Yeah. Yeah." Roddy rolled his eyes and walked away.

"Do you know where they plan to film?"

"Not yet. Should find out here in a few days though."

"Hopefully we can finish the tour."

"To hell with the tour."

"What do you mean? Q, we have been working for this for years. We've finally made it." I sighed heavily, my headache returning.

There was truth in what he said.

I had clawed my way from the shit-filled gutters of L.A. to be here.

"Yeah, I suppose you're right."

"Well, the good news is, that while you are off living like a Hollywood star, I will be here with the band working on some new music for the album."

"You better send me all the goods while I'm gone."

"I got you. I might need you to record some stuff while you're gone." I clapped his shoulder.

"You got it, bro."

"I can't wait to see who your leading lady is."

"I heard a rumor that it's going to be Marina."

"From Diocese?"

"The very same."

"Dude, that would be awesome, you two would kill those roles together."

"Fingers crossed." There was a shuffle behind me, and I turned my head to look over my shoulder as Barry peeked in.

The redhead from the night before stood naked behind me.

There was a shift in my groin.

My stomach tightened.

"Are you coming back to bed?" she asked. I smirked slightly, my headache instantly going away. I looked back at Barry.

"Get the guys together, we're going to celebrate later. Right now, I have a civic duty to uphold." Barry smirked and with a nod, walked down the hall towards Trevor's room. I closed the door and turned my full attention to the voluptuous woman before me.

A growl emanated from my chest as I threw my hand around her throat. A gasp of arousal escaped her lips. Heat surged through me. My dick stiffened at the sound she made. I moved my hand up, pushing my thumb into her mouth, grazing her teeth as she looked up at me with eyes filled with desire.

"Good girl."

Chapter 3

Lisey

The email came within three days and here I was just a few hours later, packed and sitting at LAX, waiting to board my flight to Scotland.

"Do you have your passport?" Mom asked as I scrambled to get my things together.

"Yes. It's in my purse."

"Rain jacket?"

"Yes, mom." I turned and she placed her hands on my shoulders, rubbing them up and down my arms.

"You are going to do well, my dear girl. I am so incredibly proud of you." I smiled as she leaned in and kissed my forehead.

"Thanks mom."

My leg bounced anxiously now as I waited for them to call for boarding. When the email said that we were going to be filming in Scotland, I was surprised, but also excited, that meant that dad and I could meet up during downtime for the film.

"Now boarding first class for this evening's flight to London." I looked at my ticket and sure enough, they had booked me first class. I stood from my chair and smoothed out the skirt of my dress, grabbing my purse, I walked over to get in line to board.

As I found my seat, I sat down, they had me in the window seat, which I was thankful for. I pulled my recent read from my purse and immediately stuck my nose into it.

The sounds of clasps of overhead bins closing, drifted away as I lost myself in the dark romance of The Wraith.

It was a bump against my foot that pulled me from my book, and I looked up, into dark blue eyes belonging to a man with dark hair.

"Sorry," he grumbled. He seemed as though he had just woken up.

"No problem," I said quietly. He nodded and then proceeded to throw a bag in the compartment above my head, before taking the seat next to me. I glanced back down at my book, aching to return to a world that wasn't my own.

"What are you reading?" My eyes flicked up to his and he was eyeing the cover of the book as I held it in my hands.

"The Wraith," I replied.

"Is it any good?"

"So far."

"What's it about?"

"A young woman who falls in love with the soul of a damned man." My response was short, and I watched him shift uncomfortably. I marked my page and put the book back in my purse. "I'm sorry, I get a little nervous when I fly." I held my hand out. "I'm Lisey." He took my hand in his and shook it firmly, a glint in his eyes.

"I'm Q."

"Just the letter?" I asked. He chuckled slightly.

"For now." He smirked.

"What takes you to London?" I asked.

"A layover." I rolled my eyes as a laugh escaped me.

"Where are you going?" I asked.

"Edinburgh."

"Same." He looked at me curiously.

"What is taking you to Edinburgh?"

"Work. You?"

"Same," he replied with a slight groan, before locking eyes with me. I cleared my throat and adjusted my glasses. "Ironic, you are reading about wraiths, on a flight to Edinburgh."

"Ironic how?"

"Wraiths are legendary in Scotland."

"I guess, I never really looked into them that much."

"You're more interested in the love story."

"More or less." I felt my cheeks turn red as I replayed some of the contents of the book in my mind. It was more than just a love story, there was dark, passionate content that I was not going to detail to a stranger on a fourteen-hour flight. My eyes traced up to his and there was a hint of humor in his eyes. He noticed the blush on my cheeks and a small smirk played at the corner of his lips.

His eyes slowly began trailing down from my eyes to my lips and then further down. A sudden heat began inside me, and I cleared my throat again before turning my gaze out the window. There was no way, I was being turned on watching this exceptionally fine man I had just met, eye me up and down.

I sighed heavily. I had dealt with men looking at me that way for years, but none of them ever made my body react this way. There was a silence between us, and I became curious. I turned my head to look at him and found his head back against the headrest, his eyes closed. Thick JBL headphones on his head. The faint sound of a heavy song could be heard ever so slightly in the quiet. There was static over the PA, and then the ding of an oncoming announcement.

"Attention passengers, British Airways, welcomes you this evening." I tuned it out; he didn't so much as budge.

Feeling embarrassed, I turned my head back to the window and watched as gentle raindrops began to hit the glass.

CHAPTER 4

Quinn

I had barely made it to the airport in time to beat TSA and get to my flight. The night out I had with the boys after the last show of the tour, was a long and drunken one, that ended with me bringing home an enticing blonde from the bar.

They scanned my ticket, and I rushed on to the plane as they were getting ready to board the final group. I wanted to get to my seat and get comfortable. I hated flying, most of our tour we would travel by bus, unless it was absolutely unavailable.

I found my seat with ease and was stopped suddenly as my eyes landed on a head full of chestnut soft curls. I looked up again to make sure that this was the right seat and to my delight it was. I stepped closer and my foot hit something. Looking down, I realized that I had just kicked her foot with my own. Excellent job, Q. I scolded myself. She looked up, her eyes were a rich green, like emeralds, framed with thick black glasses, her lips a pale pink, set in a pout that started a fire in my groin. Oh, the things that I could do to that mouth.

"Sorry," I grumbled, slightly embarrassed. Her green eyes were set, as though she was reading something that had her hot and bothered and I had interrupted.

"No problem." Her voice was quiet, a very slight hint of irritation behind it. I had disturbed her. I put my bag in the compartment above and then took my seat next to her, checking out the cover of her book.

"What are you reading?" I really didn't care what she was reading, I wanted to get her attention.

"The Wraith," she replied as her eyes met mine. I looked into them, she was not happy that she was being bothered, but I didn't care, I had seen that look in the eyes of many woman before and somehow, I was always able to get them into my bed. This, however, could be promising for the mile high club. I felt a smirk riding at the corner of my mouth at the thought of nailing this girl in the bathroom, forty thousand feet above the ground.

"What's it about?"

"A young woman who falls in love with the soul of a damned man." I shifted in my seat. The romance type wasn't really my bag, but for a quick hit, it didn't matter. She was feisty and that I could work with. She closed the book and leaned over to put it back in her bag. I watched as he shoulder blades shifted under her tight blouse, feeling the heat in my groin grow as I imagined them bare, flexing as I fucked her from behind. She sat back up and locked eyes with me. "I'm sorry, flying makes me anxious." She held her hand out to me.

"I'm Lisey." I wasn't big on names; it usually didn't matter by the time the sun came up. I took her hand and shook it.

"I'm Q."

"Just the letter?" she replied sarcastically.

"For now." She laughed slightly and I could feel my member growing in my pants. It was a good thing that I opted for a pair of baggy sweatpants for the long flight.

"What takes you to London?" she asked.

"A layover." She laughed again and something coiled deep in my stomach. Her laugh was soft, bringing back a flicker of innocence I had long forgotten.

"Where are you going?"

"Edinburgh."

"Same." My lips curved slightly, the possibilities of getting under her skirt just got greater, with such a long flight, a layover and then another flight, there was no doubt in my mind that I would have this girl begging for more by the time this journey ended.

"What takes you to Edinburgh?" I wanted to know how long she planned to be there. I was easily going to be there for a few months; filming was set to stay in place for at least twelve weeks before moving to Canada.

"Work. You?" Ah the little minx, giving such a simplified answer.

"Same." The silence was quick to follow, but I had to keep this conversation going.

"Ironic you are reading about wraiths on a flight to Edinburgh."

"Ironic how?" I didn't know much about the paranormal, but I had looked up interesting things about Scotland on the ride to the airport.

"They are legendary in Scotland."

"I guess, I never really looked into them."

"You are more interested in the love story."

"More or less." Her eyes were locked with mine, now was the time to change the game. I traced my eyes down towards her pouty lips, further down her perfectly accentuated neck, to her perky, well-rounded breasts. She turned her gaze away from me and my eyes snapped back up to her as she looked out the window. She was either disgusted or intrigued. I felt a smile creasing at the corners of my mouth and reached for the headphones around my neck, pulling them over my ears, playing our latest track, before resting my head back and closing my eyes.

It was her shifting in the seat next to me, that I could feel her eyes on me. That's right baby, I have you hooked.

CHAPTER 5

Lisey

A s the plane landed in London, Q quickly
grabbed his stuff from overhead and stood

back, stopping the line of people behind him, so I could exit the row.

"Thank you."

"See you at the next gate," he said. A charming smile appeared on his face. I nodded casually and walked down the aisle, exiting the plane.

As I walked off the jet bridge, I pulled my phone from my purse and turned the airplane mode off. It was eleven-forty. I quickly opened my contacts.

The phone rang several times before his business voice echoed from the end of the line.

"Lis, have you arrived?"

"Yeah, Dad. I just landed."

"How was the flight?" I looked over my shoulder as I saw Q. He had just emerged from the bridge, glancing at me and throwing me a wink before disappearing into the terminal.

The feeling in my stomach returned and I shook it off.

"It was fine."

"Did you get any sleep?"

"A little bit."

"When does your next flight leave?"

I peered over the crowd looking for Q.

"In a few hours," I replied absently.

"What are you going to do in the meantime?"

My stomach gurgled as his question hit my ears.

"Probably grab something to eat. I'm starving."

"Well, you have a nip for your dear ole Dad, yeah?"

"Will do," I laughed.

"Alright, my darling. Text me before your flight leaves and call me when you get to Edinburgh. I called your cousin Archibold, he can't wait to see you. I know you won't be out to the highlands for a few weeks, but it's been a while since you saw the family there."

"I know. I look forward to seeing them all. It's nice that the film is being done close to them."

"Talk soon." His voice clipped as a phone rang in the background.

"I love you." It came out small almost childlike. Like all those times when I was younger and he rushed to get off the phone.

"Cheers." His same goodbye as always. Made me wonder if he loved me at all, or if I was just the mistake that kept trying to hold on to him.

The call ended and I looked around. The first thing I needed to do was find the bathroom and then I would have to call Mom and let her know that I made it, and then I'd find somewhere to get lunch.

Exiting the restroom, I realized looking at the arrival and departure screen that my flight was leaving out of the same terminal.

"That's convenient," I said. I began walking down the hall, until I found, without a hint of irony, an Irish pub and to no one's surprise, Q was already seated at the bar with a pint in front of him. The scent of fried food filled my senses, making my stomach growl again.

I looked around for another place to sit, but as it was the middle of the day, most of the seats were taken. Except for one barstool right next to him. I sighed and walked in.

"Is this seat taken?" I asked. He looked up from his phone and a smile spread across his lips. The unfamiliar heat returned at his smile.

"No, it's all yours." He stood and pulled the stool out for me, gently pushing it back towards the bar as I sat down. He sat down beside me. As he rested his hands on the bar, my eyes followed the intricate tattoos covering them, disappearing into the sleeves of his hoodie.

"Drink?"

"What?" My brain hadn't grasped what he had said. My eyes were on his lips, as they moved the words didn't register.

His question startled me, and I felt my face grow hot.

"Would you like a drink?" he asked. My eyes locked with his and I couldn't tell if he had seen that I was checking out his ink. I nodded.

"Can I get a..." He looked at me and smirked. "Glass of white wine for the lady?" he said to the barkeep.

"Actually, I'll have a whiskey," I replied. The bartender looked at me and nodded before turning away to get my drink.

"Whiskey girl?" He cocked an eyebrow at me.

"I like the hard stuff." The bartender put the glass down in front of me and I threw it back without so much as a cough or choke. I could feel Q's eyes on me.

"Can we get the lady another one please?" The bartender nodded.

"Would you like a menu?" he asked before he walked away.

"Yes, please." He pulled one from behind the bar and placed it down in front of me. I picked up the menu and gazed down at it, keeping myself from looking up at Q, though I could feel him watching me. I knew better than to engage in such a way with someone I had just met. I had already broken my mother's golden travel rules.

You never tell them where you are going.

You never tell them why you are travelling.

The only people who knew I was working on this were my parents, my boss and the people that hired me. I still hadn't even seen the cast list yet.

"Anything look good?" he asked.

His voice snapped me out of my thoughts.

I peered over the edge of the menu at him. His deep blue eyes locked with mine.

"Still trying to decide." He smirked slightly and then took a swig of the beer that he held in his hand. I don't know when he had finished the first one, but I could clearly tell that this one was fresh. I watched him drink, his throat constricting as he swallowed. I felt my cheeks warming and instantly looked away. He set the beer down and I felt his eyes on me once more.

"Try the beans and toast if you aren't sure." His voice was like silk as he spoke and I nodded, absentmindedly closing the menu and putting it down.

"Sounds great," I said with a slight laugh. I picked up the shot in front of me and once again downed it in one gulp, the heat reaching into my core as my head began to spin slightly.

CHAPTER 6

Quinn

I took a seat at the first bar that I found. She had worked me over by simply being in the same air space as me and I needed a drink to bring myself back down to earth.

"What will it be?" the bartender asked.

"A pint of your finest lager please." The bartender knocked on the bar twice with a nod and walked away. I looked out into the crowded hallway, in some way I hoped she would find me here, but on the other hand I didn't care either way. She was clearly amused by me in some way, and I made her blush, which brought devious thoughts to mind. Like how my hand would feel around that delicate neck of hers.

The glass hitting the bar broke me from my thoughts, thankfully as I felt my member beginning to rise from its slumber with eagerness. I picked up the glass and began to chug it. Downing it almost as quickly as it had been set before me. Setting the glass down the bartender eyed me, suspiciously.

"That kind of day lad?" His Irish accent was thick, surprising really being as we were in London.

"You could say that."

"Is it a woman?" he asked. I fingered the lip of the glass as a smirk played at the corner of my lips.

"Could say that too." My eyes met his and he glanced out of the bar into the hallway.

"Well, I'll get you another one then," he said with a nod. He walked away and I turned my head and sure enough there was the luscious woman herself, standing there looking for a place to sit. I picked up my phone and kept my eyes on it, looking for something to keep my eyes from wandering back to her.

"Is this seat taken?"

I looked up as she stood feet away from me. Our eyes locking. I put my phone down.

"No, it's all yours," I said as I held my hand out to the empty barstool available next to me. She seemed hesitant as she closed the small space between us. I stood from my seat and pulled it out, allowing her to sit before I gently pushed it back against the bar. Women love that romantic crap. I took my seat next to her.

"Can we get a," I looked her up and down, my eyes lingering on her low v-cut blouse as her cleavage was nearly begging for attention. I cleared my throat. "A glass of white wine for the lady?" I said.

"Actually, I'll have whiskey." I cocked my eyebrow, and my eyes locked with hers. Her thick framed glasses did nothing to hide how stunning she was.

"Whiskey girl?"

"I like the hard stuff," she replied. I felt my lip twitch as my eyebrow cocked. My stomach knotted.

As the bartender returned she took the shot glass that was set before her and downed the whiskey without so much as a flinch. Something stirred inside of me.

Something dark.

Something feral.

There was something exceptionally hot about a woman who could handle whiskey. It wasn't a drink that one would find many refined ladies to indulge in.

And this girl was refined.

Behind those glasses she was hot.

And she knew it.

I turned to the bartender.

"Can we get another for the lady, please?" The bartender nodded and then turned to her.

"Would you like a menu?"

"Yes, please." Her voice was delicate, the faint hint of the whiskey on her breath.

Intoxicating.

The bartender handed her a menu; she opened it completely blocking me from seeing her face. I smirked and turned my attention back to the beer in front of me. She was embarrassed, which meant that the odds were still turning in my favor to bed this girl.

After a while it seemed as though she was having a tough time deciding, the bartender had returned with her shot, and she left it untouched on the bar.

"Try the beans and toast, if you aren't sure, it's good." She put the menu down and regarded me silently, before nodding her head. The bartender returned and she placed her order. As he walked away she took the shot in front of her and threw it back as fast as the first one. I looked at the bartender.

"Another please." Lisey looked up at me and shook her head.

"No, I couldn't."

"Why not? It's not like you are flying a plane or something." A smile tugged at my lips, but I could see it in her eyes, her cheeks now flush. I signaled the bartender for a water, sliding it toward her without fanfare. I wanted her, but not if she was too far gone to choose it. Most of the drunken women I took to my bed would have already decided. Lisey, I couldn't quite read. She was playing the quiet and romantic type, but something told me this girl had a wild side. I was determined to bring that out, even if it meant a slow approach.

I looked at my phone to distract myself; we would need to board our next plane within the hour.

CHAPTER 7

Lisey

B y the time my food arrived, my head was swimming, it was almost as though I had downed an entire bottle of champagne in just a few drinks. I was happy when the beans and toast arrived, it was honestly one of my favorite breakfast items. When I came to visit my dad, he made sure that was on every morning menu.

"My American girl, having beans and toast for breakfast."

"It's good."

"Wouldn't you prefer waffles or pancakes."

"I can have that home; I'm here for the experience."

The conversation played over in my mind as I quietly began to eat, my first trip to see dad after he settled. I was eight. I used to love coming to visit him, until that she devil came into his life.

"How is it?" My reverie broke as Q's voice boomed over my thoughts.

"It's actually one of my favorites."

"Oh really? Do you travel to London often?"

"Not as much as I used to, my father actually lives here." I watched as his eyebrows raised in surprise.

"You aren't going to see him while you are here?"

"It's a two-hour layover. Besides, I'll be in Edinburgh for a little while, we are planning to get together at some point."

"So, you said, you were going to Edinburgh to work." I nodded, with that now back at the forefront of my mind, I realized I needed to slow down on the whiskey, I was set to meet with the assistant director the moment that I arrived.

"I am."

"What is it you do?" I wasn't allowed to talk about the movie, and my mother's voice began to ring in my head.

"Never tell a stranger you meet while traveling what you are there for, be vague, it will keep you safe. There are so many traffickers out there these days." I pushed her voice away.

Blinking, he was still focused on me. Waiting for an answer.

"I'm a writer," I blurted.

"A writer?" I nodded as I stuffed the last bite of food into my mouth.

"What do you write?"

"I'm here to do a research piece on Highlander Architecture." The lie came out so smoothly, I almost believed it myself. If I weren't dressed like a secretary then I'm sure he wouldn't believe me, but this was the way I liked it, low key, one glamour pop and everyone who knew anything about fashion, or modeling, including the paparazzi would recognize me right away as Elenor Fitz's daughter.

"What about you?" I asked pushing away the thought.

"I'm a musician."

"Trying to make it famous in Edinburgh?" He cocked his eyebrow at me, with intrigue. "What?"

"Nothing." I elbowed him gently as the whiskey had now taken over almost all of my poise and common sense.

"What?" I asked with a giggle. He took his beer and sipped it before putting it back down. He cracked a smile at me.

"I've just never met a girl like you before." I rolled my eyes, what a cliché response.

"Well, I've never heard of an aspiring musician going to Edinburgh. London it's where it's at. You have the Beatles, Elton John, The Clash, Coldplay."

"No." I looked at him startled as he interrupted me. "Not Coldplay," he laughed.

"Alright, but still there are so many great bands and musicians that came out of London. You were literally in LA, why would you come all the way out here?" My question seemed to catch him off guard as he picked up his glass and downed the rest of his drink. The bartender put a receipt in front of him, and he signed it, before putting his card back in his wallet. I didn't even notice that he had asked for his bill. He stood from his chair and held his hand out to me.

"Shall we? Our flight boards in fifteen minutes."

"I have to get my bill first."

"I paid it." I reached for my purse.

"Let me pay you back. I can't accept that." As
I reached inside of it, his hand touched mine,
shooting a spark straight through my fingers, up
my arm, through my body like lightning. He must
have felt it too, because he quickly pulled away,
releasing my hand.

"That's not necessary."

"I can't let you pa."

"But I already did," he interrupted. My eyes
locked with his.

"Thank you." He nodded and pulled the stool
out for me to stand. I got to my feet, and they felt
like Jello, the whiskey going straight to my head.
The room spun a little bit, and the lightning feeling sparked through my body again as he grabbed
my elbow.

"Whoa there." I straightened myself, embarrassed.

"I'm sorry." I felt my cheeks turning red and I wasn't sure anymore if it was from the whiskey or from the sheer embarrassment I was feeling.

"Don't be. Come on, let's get to the gate." I nodded and he linked his arm with mine, leading me down the hallway towards our gate.

As they called for boarding, Q, let me go to walk ahead, following close behind me as we were both seated in first class.

When we got on the plane I took my seat, next to the window in the third row as he continued to his window seat in the row across from me.

It wasn't long before an older gentleman took the seat next to me and was preparing to settle in comfortably. I glanced across the aisle to Q, who's eyes darkened as the man sat next to me. Suddenly, to my surprise, he stood up and spilled out into the aisle.

CHAPTER 8

Quinn

"Excuse me sir," I said quietly to the man sitting next to Lisey. He looked up at me with weary eyes.

"Would you be interested in taking the window seat across the aisle?" The man looked across the aisle at my vacant seat, before looking up at me again.

"I'm not trying to inconvenience you sir, but you see, she's my traveling partner and we were seated separately somehow."

He turned his gaze to look at her, and I could feel a fire of envy burning in my chest.

He looked back at me, which for his sake he was lucky.

Had he dared to glance at her even a little bit longer and I may have lost all of my senses and ripped him from the seat.

He nodded and began to get up.

I looked at Lisey and gave her a slight smile as she peered up at me through her lashes, behind those glasses she wore.

Everything was falling into place, she was very much interested, and I was determined to have her in my bed by the end of the night, maybe more than once.

"You okay?" she asked.

"Yeah, why?" My response breathless.

"You seemed amped up for a second there." I didn't realize she had noticed, but I was glad that her eyes were focused on my face and not the growth of my cock in my sweatpants. A small smile creeped into the corner of my lips.

"All good."

"Are you sure?" I thought it was adorable. She was so concerned, and she had only met me last night when we boarded the flight to LAX. It almost pulled at me a little bit. Of course she had to be sexy as fuck, in a hot nerdy, librarian sort of way. Just another fling in my extensive line of woman that I'd had since we got big. Before that I could barely get a single girl to come home with me, but money and fame talk. It surprised me actually that she had been sitting next to me this entire time and had no idea who I was. That got me curious.

"What kind of music do you like?" I asked.

"Classical mostly."

"Really?"

"Yeah, I know it sounds weird, but it helps me really focus on my writing."

"Are you working on something besides your piece in Scotland?" She cleared her throat and pushed her glasses up on her face nervously.

"Kinda."

"What are you working on?"

"My debut novel."

"Oh, really?" She nodded sheepishly.

"Let me guess, it's a romance?" She cocked her eyebrows at me before rolling her eyes. Something possessive rose in me, I wanted nothing more than to grab her chin, forcing her to look at me. Women rolling their eyes at me, always set something feral off inside of me.

My stomach tightened. I didn't know how much longer I would be able to hold it before I just took her into the bathroom. It was that moment; she bit her lip, and I was gripping the seat with my entire ass. This girl knew exactly what she was doing and she either learned it from her books or from experience.

I didn't give a single shit to know how she knew but I liked it, and I wanted more of her, right here, right now. I grabbed her chin and pulled her face close to mine, her eyes widened behind her glasses, up close I could see how emerald, green they were.

Captivating.

"Don't," I said breathlessly.

"What?" Her voice emanated a feign innocence that drove me mad.

"Don't bite your lip."

Almost on impulse or instinct, she bit her lip again, challenging me.

I felt my fingers tense slightly against her delicate skin, careful to retain myself so as to not bruise her beautiful face. The heat inside of me roared, but I forced a breath through my nose. Not here. Not like this. She deserved more than to be ruined in a cramped plane bathroom. Her eyes were pleading with me to continue, but I had to control the urge to take her here and now in front of everyone on this damn plane.

I put my mouth close to hers and her eyes closed. Grazing my lips ever so slightly against her pouty plump mouth, a breath hitching in her throat, fueling the blaze inside me. I gently pulled her face down and planted a soft kiss on her forehead, before releasing her. Her eyes fluttered open, and she sat back in her seat, her chest heaving.

I could have kicked my own ass in that moment. Everything was where it needed to be, except the location. Part of me wanted to take her by the hand and lead her to the lavatory, but now we were taxiing down the runway, the plane gaining speed, pinning us back in our seats.

As we got into the air and the plane leveled out, I looked at her, and her eyes were still on me. There was something in them, a light of some sort that held my gaze with hers. I shifted in my seat, closer to her. Her chest rising and falling with anticipation.

At some point I must have fallen asleep. Waking up when I heard the word descent come over the PA. I felt something heavy on my arm and looked over to find Lisey, her soft curls draped down my arm as she slept on my shoulder. I sighed heavily. The plane would land soon, and I would probably never see her again.

As the plane teetered above the ground, she remained sleeping until the tires hit the tarmac, jolting her awake. My arm across her chest, caressing her thigh, as well as hold her back in her seat. As she stirred I retrieved my arm.

The seatbelt light turned off, we silently stood, but I could feel her eyes locked on me as I grabbed my bag from the overhead bin. I glanced over her quickly, before blocking the throng of people that were making their way down the aisle to the front.

"Thank you." She was quiet as she stepped ahead of me and headed toward the front of the plane.

CHAPTER 9

Lisey

My mind was reeling. The way he had grabbed my face had sent fire purging through my body, something that I was unfamiliar with. My reaction to biting my lips as he asked me not to felt as though I was disobeying a command, and it was exhilarating, sending prickles up my entire body. Part of me wanted him to go further, but I had never so much as kissed a boy, let alone been touched by one. I felt my cheeks go red, but he was so close to my face I don't think he even noticed.

As he let me go, my chest was heaving with anticipation. He looked like he was upset with himself in some way, like there was more that he wanted to say, or more that he wanted to do.

I felt the speed of the plane pick up, throwing me back against my seat as I continued to watch him, waiting to see if he was going to say something. My eyelids were heavy, and before I knew it, darkness had already claimed me.

***

It was a sudden jolt that woke me, and I briefly felt, Q's hand slide across my lap as he took his arm away from across me. I looked at him briefly, but his eyes were set on the stewardess who was now standing at the front of the plane saying something over the PA. I didn't hear her, all I wanted was to ask him why he had stopped, as the memories of what had transpired came to the forefront of my mind.

As the plane began to disembark, he got out once again into the aisle and grabbed his bag, stopping traffic so I could get out of my seat. I stood, pulling my purse over my shoulder and nodded at him gently.

"Thank you." He didn't say a word, and I turned with my head down, making my way off of the plane. With every step I was beating myself up. It was probably just some twisted dream I had, from reading all of those romance novels, but if that were the case, then why could I still feel his hand tight on my face?

Exiting the bridge, I didn't dare turn back around as embarrassment had flooded me. He was kind enough to pay for my lunch and to entertain me along the trip, but now it was time to get serious.

"You didn't work hard to go nowhere, Ellisia Hammond," I scolded myself. I picked up the pace as I made my way down the hallway, towards the baggage claim. I didn't have much time before my ride from the production company would arrive.

"Lisey." I stopped, turning around as Q was striding up behind me, he seemed taller somehow after our encounter or dream encounter whatever it may have been.

"Yes?" I felt something tightening in my stomach as he stopped in front of me, towering over.

"You forgot this." I looked down and in his hand was my book.

"Oh. I didn't even realize it had fallen out of my bag." I looked up my eyes locking with his. "Thank you."

"You're welcome." I wrapped my arms tightly around the book, clutching it to my chest as I turned and walked away. When I peeked back over my shoulder, Q had already disappeared into the crowd.

As I found my carousel, I kept my eyes on the round track, trying to keep from looking for him. It was then I was gratefully distracted by the shrill ringing of my phone. I fished it from my purse and answered it before seeing who it was.

"Hello?"

"Lisey, honey, have you landed in Scotland?"

"Yes, Mom."

"Have you met with your driver yet?" I looked around a group of drivers with signs hung near the exit.

"Not yet, I'm still waiting on my bag."

"Have you heard from the production team?"

"No, why?"

"The cast list came out today, an official one, from Whiplash Productions."

"Really?"

"Yes, the young man playing Ayaan Lawson, is a rockstar from a band called Nitrous Ruin."

Of course it was. I rolled my eyes.

If there was anything I remembered from my set days, it was that rock stars were the most arrogant.

"Sounds like a band I will never listen to."

"And the female lead is Marina from a band called Diocese."

"Interesting." I faintly heard what she was telling me as my eyes lingered over and found Q standing along the wall, waiting for the same carousel.

"Honey, are you even listening to me?" I snapped back to the conversation.

"Yeah, Nitrous Ruin and Diocese."

"They are gaining popularity, and the young man is quite a looker." I felt a weird tinge in my stomach at her words.

"Mom." I sighed, a hidden disgust in my voice.

"What? I can have an opinion can't I?"

"Yeah, but still."

"Anyway, I have to run darling, Hiram has a photoshoot set up for this afternoon and I have to get ready. I pulled the phone away and looked at the time, it was just past three in the afternoon.

"What time is the shoot?"

"Twelve thirty?"

"You need five hours to get ready?"

"Perfection takes time, my love."

"Alright, well I'll text you when I get back from my meeting with the assistant director."

"Sounds great love, knock them dead." I smiled and the phone call ended. I put my phone back in my purse. I didn't even notice that the carousel had already begun, and bags were coming off from the plane. I looked around and sure enough my bag was already on the other side. I began towards it, my heels desperately clicking as I made my way across the tile floor in a flurry.

Someone walked right in front of me and their bag contacted my foot, sending me forward toward the floor.

The tile gleamed in the lights as I crashed towards it.

A strong arm shot out of nowhere, steadying me, before anyone really noticed what had happened. My eyes flicked up to see Q, he looked down at me, his eyes dark and broody. He released my arm and raced over to the carousel, retrieving my bag. He placed it in front of me.

"Are you always this clumsy?" he asked with a smirk on his face.

"Only on my best days," I laughed as I picked up my bag.

He didn't ask. Instead, he reached out and took my bag from me as he had his own bag and guitar slung over his shoulder.

"You really don't have to; I can get it."

"Where are you headed?" he asked ignoring me entirely.

"I have a ride." I nodded my head towards the group of drivers that I had spotted earlier.

"Let's find your ride." He walked past me without giving me any room to argue. I followed him toward the crowd of drivers that had accumulated nearby. One driver held a sign with my last name scrawled across it, standing closer to the edge of the group. I watched as Q walked right up to him, then curiosity struck me. I had never told him my full name.

CHAPTER 10

Quinn

As she walked off the plane, I saw her duck her head down. I blew my chance with this one and it was going to gnaw at me. I usually didn't care much for conquest, but this one was far more intriguing and harder to conquer. As I took a step to follow her, something caught my eye. I looked down and, just under the seat in front of where she had been sitting, was her book, The Wraith. I ducked into the row quickly, retrieving it, before backing out. Looking up, she had already exited the plane, and several others had taken my distraction as an opportunity to move forward. I lingered in the line impatiently waiting.

When I got off the plane, I found myself looking over the afternoon, until I spotted her soft curls, strutting away in the distance. I quickly pulled one of my business cards from my pocket and shoved it in where she had her place marked in the book. I might kick myself in the ass for that later, I never gave my number to any of the girls I slept with or planned to sleep with. I was leaving the ball in her court; she could do with it as she wished.

"Lisey." I called. I approached her quickly, practically in front of her before she turned around completely, her eyes locking with mine.

"Yes." It came out innocent, sending a shockwave through my body, making the impulse to grab her around the waist and pull her towards me hard to fight.

"You forgot this." I held up her book. Gently she took it from me, wrapping her arms around it and holding it tightly to her chest.

"I didn't even realize it had fallen out of my bag. Thank you."

"You're welcome." Before I could string together a single coherent sentence, she turned and was walking away once more. I stepped out of the crowd and headed off to the side, to call Roddy and Barry, to let them know I had made it. I kept my eyes on her as the phone rang, and I noticed how she turned and looked back, her eyes scanning the crowd. There was still hope for me yet.

I was at the carousel, leaning against the wall, waiting for my bag as I watched her. Her book now tucked in her purse as she was on the phone with someone. I tried to make out what she was saying but couldn't get a good enough read. It could be a friend, a boyfriend. The thought made me laugh a little. No matter, I had slept with many girls who were married or had boyfriends, I wasn't proud of it, but a lady wants what a lady wants, and I am a man that will deliver.

The carousel began to move, and I saw my bag come up quickly, followed by my guitar. I reached for them and noticed that the bag that came out next to it had a name scribbled on the tag. Ellisia Hammond. I backed away from the turning track and leaned once more against the wall, watching her as she was one her phone.

As her phone call ended, I saw the immediate shock on her face as her eyes fell on the bag that had come out next to mine. I began to make my way over to her quickly. Just in time as she stumbled over someone who had cut her off with their bag, my arm reaching out, grabbing her, and steadying her before she hit the floor. Before she could say anything, I hurriedly walked over and grabbed her bag for her.

Returning, I set it down in front of her.

"Are you always this clumsy?" I asked, with a smirk. She rolled her eyes at me and the heat coiled in my stomach once more.

"Only on my best days," she laughed. A hint of embarrassment reddening her cheeks. She picked up her bag.

Without a word, I reached out and took the bag from her.

"You don't have to do that; I can get it."

"Where are you heading?" I asked, ignoring her.

"I have a ride." She nodded towards a group by the exit. I walked past her towards a group of drivers that I had seen when I came down from the upper level, several of them were holding signs and right away I saw one with the name Rose on it.

Near them was another one that said Hammond.
I walked over to the one that had her last name on
it.

"This is Miss Hammond," I said. The driver
nodded and put the sign down before he took her
bag from me. I turned to find my driver, and she
was standing behind me. Her emerald eyes locked
with mine that made it hard for me to move.

"Thank you," she said quietly.

"You're welcome."

"Goodbye, Q." Something in her words felt final and I didn't like the way it made me feel. I had a
lot of fun on this journey with her and was hoping
for so much more, but I blew my chances. My only
hope now was that she would find the card in her
book.

"Good luck with your piece on Highland Architecture."

"Good luck with your music." A soft smile appeared on her lips.

"Goodbye, Lisey." She dropped her gaze before brushing past me lightly and following her driver to a waiting car, just outside the door.

"Mr. Rose, I presume?" I turned my head and there stood another driver, looking at me as he held a sign with my name on it.

"That's me." He held out his hand, and I let him take my luggage from me.

"Right this way, sir." I nodded and followed him down the hall a little ways, before exiting, where a large black SUV sat waiting at the curb.

CHAPTER 11

Lisey

"I saw the cast list today." Aggie was practically screaming in my ear.

"My mom called and told me about it, some rockstar I guess is playing the lead."

"Not just any rockstar, Quinn Rose."

"Never heard of him."

"Lisey, you can't be serious, he's hot and up and coming. Heard he's a bit of a ladies man as well."

"Well, you know me."

"Yeah, yeah, if it isn't Beethoven, Yanni or Mozart, you aren't interested," she interrupted.

"Am I that predictable?" I asked sarcastically.

"Yes!" she exclaimed.

"Well, I like what I like."

"You can't tell me you don't think that this man is fine as fuck?"

"I have never seen him before and mind yourself, you aren't even supposed to know that I'm working on this project," I said, keeping my voice low.

"I know, but still, girl, wake up, you are twenty-four years old, you are in another country on your own, with a fine ass man for several weeks working on a movie." I scoffed at her words.

"Like some big, up and coming rockstar would take much interest in me."

"Lose the librarian look. You and I both know you are hot as hell, bitch." I smiled slightly as I pushed my glasses up my face as they had slid down the bridge of my nose. No one but a few people knew that they were prop glasses, I never really needed them, but they helped feed the "librarian" look that Aggie referred to.

"Aggie, we have been friends since we were tots, you know that I only dress like this to separate myself from my mother."

"I know, but babe, hear me out. You are in Scotland; there can't be that many people that would put two and two together. Get your sexy ass dressed up and get out there and find yourself a good lay. It may not be the rockstar, but damn girl, get some ass." I laughed at her as she spoke excitedly.

"Can't I just hang out with a book and a good cup of tea."

"No. Get your fine ass out there and get yourself some dick." The thought of letting a man touch my naked body sent a shiver down my spine.

"I don't know, Aggie."

"Don't make me call the press."

"You wouldn't?" I said something resembling fear clawed into my throat.

"I will if you don't get out of those drab clothes and into something more fitting."

"Aggie."

"Don't, Aggie me," she interrupted. I felt the pressure of her words through the phone. I always had been recluse, trying to fend off the modeling agency for years as they tried to pull me into their realm, to follow my mother's legacy. Aggie was the only person in the world who knew me better than I knew myself, almost like a sister more so than a best friend, she was only pushing because she wanted me to get out of my shell. A memory came flooding back in that moment, of the last time that she convinced me to go out after getting all dressed up.

We had walked into Warwick, an elite and up-scale club in the heart of LA. It wasn't long before the paparazzi caught up and ambushed us as we were trying to go to the ladies room. Somehow they had snuck through security with a hidden camera and bombarded us. The next day, my face was plastered on the front cover of several news outlets. Mom was furious. The title, 'Model Cit-izen?.' I remember how she had tossed the paper at me the next morning, as I was icing a bruise on my thigh. A souvenir from crashing into a table, trying to escape the man with a million questions and a camera.

"Lis?" My mind snapped back from the memo-ry and pole vaulted me back into the conversation.

"Yeah?"

"Where did you go?"

"Nowhere."

"Warwick?" I was silent, she always knew what I was thinking, and she didn't even have to be sitting in the room with me.

"That was a rough night."

"This isn't that. What happened that night was lacking on the securities end, they should have checked that guy better."

"But if I get in trouble over here, I could lose my job and that would be what my mother would refer to as an international scandal."

"Lis, listen to me. You are going to be fine. No one is going to know who you are out there. If they do, I doubt they will think much of it, because why would Elenor Fitz's daughter be in Edinburgh?" She had a point. I held the phone in between my shoulder and my face as I pulled my book out of my purse, looking for my wallet, so I could tip my driver, when something fell out of my book. I set it aside and picked up the little white card, turning it over, my eyes widened.

"Oh my god," the words slipped from my mouth before I could stop them.

"What?" Aggie asked.

"He gave me his number?"

"Who did?" I cleared my throat as my eyes remained on the card.

"I met someone."

"What? And you are just now telling me!"

"I met him on the flight over." Aggie suddenly changed her tune.

"No. Absolutely not. That's how you end up on the first forty-eight," Aggie said.

"He was really nice, Aggie."

"They usually start out that way and the next thing you know, they are uncovering a shallow grave with your hacked up body inside of it."

"Well, you want me to go out with complete strangers." She was silent for a minute.

"Tell me about him. I want to know everything that happened when you were with him." I sighed heavily and began at the beginning.

CHAPTER 12

Quinn

When we arrived at the hotel, I was taken aback by its massive and aged exterior. The Balmoral Hotel was a legacy, and it was immaculate as I peered upon it. My mind filtered back to Lisey and how she would have loved this for her piece on architecture. I shook the thought of her away. The way her throat moved as she swallowed flashed in my mind and I felt a tinge of excitement in my pants. I was so close, I should have just wrapped my hand around her throat and asked her to come to the hotel with me.

"Ah, welcome." I turned my mind away from her as I was immediately greeted by the assistant director.

"Mr. Rose, I'm Jafe Cambel, assistant director." He held out his hand to me, and I took it shaking it firmly, slight annoyance filling me as my cock had awoken from his slumber, now raving with desire for the girl from the plane.

"Nice to meet you, Mr. Cambel." I hid the discomfort with a smile.

"Jafe, please. We are going to be working on this project for quite some time, so we won't need the formalities." He put his hand on my shoulder and walked me inside as a bellhop immediately arrived at my side and took my bag gently from my hand. I firmly gipped the strap of my guitar case, tightening it over my shoulder.

"What's on the agenda tonight?" I asked, trying to keep my mind from where it kept trying to go.

"Tonight, we will have dinner with the production team."

"Is it something fancy?"

"In sorts, yes. If you need, I can send someone over from costumes to get you ready for the dinner."

"No, that won't be necessary, I have a suit."

"Excellent, well the cocktail hour starts, promptly at six in the grand ballroom and dinner will follow at seven thirty." I looked down at my watch. That gave me a little bit of time to clean up and take care of business before I had to show up and shmooze over the production team who had hired me.

"Sounds good." Jafe turned to me and produced a key.

"The entire team is on the top floor, so you won't have to worry about anyone disturbing you."

"Thank you." I said as I took the key.

"You will be assigned an assistant, they will be responsible for your every wish, whether it be coffee, breakfast, running errands, dry cleaning, they will be your go to and if you aren't satisfied, we will hire you a new one," Jafe said with a laugh. He seemed pompous this one, but he was paying me good money to be on this project. I laughed slightly with him and held the key up.

"Thank you, Jafe. I will see you at the reception." He nodded and briskly walked away towards the door, no doubt to light up another cigarette, as the smell practically clung to the man as though he were its lifeline. The stale smell reminded me of the times I used to sneak cigarettes from my mother, after she would pass out drunk on the couch. They would still be lit, and I would take them out back and smoke them on the steps.

As I arrived at my assigned room, looking at the key, the little tag on it read the number six-thirty-three, the bellhop was waiting patiently for me at the door. I unlocked it and opened it, he waved his hand forward, signaling for me to go first. I nodded and entered the room, immediately distracted by my phone. I pulled it from my pocket as I felt him whisk by me quickly, placing my bag on the luggage rack.

"Is there anything else you need before I take my leave, sir?" he asked. I put my phone down briefly before looking at it and set my eyes on him. He was a little guy, no more than about eighteen years old.

"No, thank you." He nodded and then proceeded to leave the room, closing the door, quietly behind him. I looked around the room briefly. It was far better than any other place that venues had booked for the band, so far.

It was the vibration that came from my phone as it sat on the dresser that reminded me that there was a text waiting for me. I picked it up and upon opening the screen, I saw Roddy's name light up.

'Make us proud, kid. We have massive things happening when you get back. Stay in touch and for the love of God, stay out of trouble.'

I rolled my eyes as I responded by sending him a thumbs up and a smiling devil face emoji, that would be sure to send him spiraling into oblivion. I backed out of his message, and another message was just below it, a number I didn't recognize, but from the area code was obviously from LA. I tapped the message, and it sprung open. A smile spread across my lips as I read the message.

'Hey Q, it's Lisey'

Reading the message, sent heat throughout my body, straight down to my groin as I relished every syllable of the message. The little minx had found my card after all, and she just served the ball back to me.

CHAPTER 13

Lisey

"**Y**ou did not just send him a text!" Aggie said through the phone.

"So, what if I did?"

"Lis, he could me an axe murderer."

"You would rather me go out and meet a random stranger on the streets of Edinburgh, than hangout with a man who is from LA?" She was silent for a moment.

"Well, if you disappear he has to come back at some point, and I'll know he did it." I laughed slightly.

"All I did was text him hi and tell him it was me, he probably won't even text back." In that moment, the car pulled up outside of the hotel. I looked out the window as the beautiful and overwhelming Balmoral Hotel, loomed over me. The door opened and I stepped out.

"Aggie. I'm going to have to call you back."

"What's going on?"

"Nothing, I just got to my hotel."

"Send pictures."

"Alright."

"Love you, bestie."

"I love you too." I ended the call and stuffed the phone back into my purse, next to my book. I was completely enamored by the majesty of the building that stood before me. It would be a perfect setting for my next novel. I would be staying here for the next several weeks, giving me plenty of time in between meetings and shooting to do some sketching.

"This way, Miss." The driver had my bag in hand and was already heading up the rounded steps towards the door.

As we walked inside, he disappeared, handing my bag off to a bellhop as a man approached me.

"Miss Hammond." He reached his hand out, taking mine in his and pulled it to his lips, kissing it gently. "Welcome to Edinburgh." I looked around the giant room, a crystal chandelier hanging in the center, vases of live flowers strategically placed around the foyer.

"Thank you, Mr."

"Jafe. Just Jafe, please, we are so happy to have you join us on this project."

"I'm happy to be here, Jafe." He held out a key to me, and I took it gently.

"The entire production is on the top floor; you shouldn't be disturbed up there."

"Thank you." I looked at the key in my hand, and the little tag said six-thirty-five.

"Cocktail hour will be at six, followed by dinner at seven-thirty."

"I will see you there." He nodded and then turned heading toward the front door.

I turned and quickly found the elevator. Walking up to it the door opened and a gentleman inside the elevator greeted me with a warm smile.

"What floor, Miss?"

"Six please." He nodded and hit the button with a gloved finger before the door closed, and the elevator gently lofted upward.

As I walked into my room, the bellhop had left my luggage on the luggage rack, before turning to me.

"Will there be anything else, Miss?"

"No, thank you." I placed my purse on the nearby dresser. He nodded and left the room. I kicked my heels off and padded across the soft carpet in my bare feet, towards the window. Throwing back the sheer curtains, I could see across Edinburgh. I pushed the window open, allowing the cool, crisp air to flow in, making the curtains dance through the room. The breeze sent a slight chill through my body, as I walked away. Letting myself fall down on the bed, the softness of the mattress enveloping me. The comfort almost pulling me straight into sleep. A yawn escaped me; I had slept a little on the plane but hadn't gotten nearly enough. My eyes began to flutter with sleep, when I suddenly heard a constant vibration coming from on the dresser. I sat up and looked at my purse as it remained where I had placed it. Groaning, I got up.

Digging to the bottom I found my phone buried inside. I pulled it free, as Dad's name appeared on the screen.

"Hey, Dad," I said as I answered the call.

"Hello, starling, did you make it to your hotel alright?"

"Yes, it's very swanky."

"Where do they have you my love?"

"Balmoral Hotel."

"Ah, yes, the Balmoral, a lovely hotel, one of the more prim and proper ones in Edinburgh."

"They definitely spared no expense; this place is fancy."

"Europeans do things a little different, ducky."

"How was work?" I knew it was pointless, but I wanted to push our conversation longer than three minutes for a change.

"As usual, meetings, schedules, all that jazz as they say." I laughed slightly as a yawn escaped me.

"Are you going to get any sleep, my dear?"

"I'm going to try." I pulled the phone away and looked at the time. "But, I have a cocktail in a few hours, and I should probably start getting ready."

"Alright, my love, I will let you go then. You'll text me tomorrow, yeah?" There was a spark in his voice.

"Of course," I said slowly.

"Alright then, don't forget to text your cousin, Archibold."

"I won't."

"Have fun at your event tonight."

"I will, Dad."

"Love you, ducky." Goosebumps raised on my skin, tingling through my body.

"I love you too."

The call ended. I looked at the time. There was enough time to squeeze in about an hour nap. I drifted back to the bed. Laying down I placed the phone on the nightstand. Barely before my fingers left it, it vibrated once more. I picked up and the number I had texted earlier lit up on the screen. My heart began to pound, I didn't think he would actually respond quickly or even at all.

'*Hello, Lisey*'

CHAPTER 14

Quinn

I was just getting out of the shower, the steam rolling out from the bathroom into the bedroom, bringing with it a slight warmth. A towel draped around my hips. I heard my phone buzzing over on the bed and padded towards it. Picking it up a smile curled in the corner of my lips.

'What's up? Did you make it to your hotel alright?'

Just as I had hoped, she was intrigued enough to keep the conversation going. I knew that the airport would not be our last encounter. I currently had no other forms of entertainment and she for now would provide for me, until I at least got the lay of the land and found some candy to keep me busy.

I walked over to the bed and sat down, kicking my legs up and resting against the head rest, my member hard as he was raised to the sky. I quickly texted her back.

'Yeah. You?'

She responded almost immediately.

'Yeah. What are you doing later?'

The question sent me sitting straight up as intrigue filled me. Why did she want to know? Did she want to get together later? Could tonight be the night?

'I have a work thing to do later, but I'm free after. Why?'

The texting bubbles popped up almost immediately and then just as quickly disappeared. My mind was wandering as my heart was racing in my chest.

I was going to do whatever it took to get out of this dinner early if she was going to agree to meet with me. I'd bring her back here, take off her little dress that she was wearing earlier and bend her over this bed. My cock twitched with anticipation.

I needed to get myself under control. The last thing I needed was to show up to a production dinner half-cocked and thinking about her mouth.

I stood up and began pacing around the room, anxiously waiting her response.

Like she could sense it.

The bubbles reappeared.

'I'm free after nine'

I quickly looked up a nearby pub. The Black Bull Tavern was nearby, just down the street from here. I texted her back.

'Black Bull Tavern, nine-thirty'

The text bubbles appeared again.

'See you there'

I walked over to the dresser, leaning against it as I looked in the mirror. Tonight was going to be the night. I had never chased after pussy this hard, but there was something about her, she had secrets that was evident, but I wanted to know what her body felt like under my touch, I wanted to know what she sounded like as I fucked her unapologetically from behind, how my hand would fit around that beautiful neck of hers. I pushed off of the dresser and headed toward the armoire to free my suit from its protective layer.

As it aired out from travel, the dark gray suit with black vest and matching tie, hung marvelously, it was the nicest thing I owned, the first thing I bought after getting paid by the record company. All my life growing up we fought to have every little scrap, and I remember one day seeing a refined gentleman walking into a fancy jewelry store, as I was selling newspapers on the corner with my brother, Henry. That day I swore I would buy myself a suit just like that and when the money hit the account, that was the first thing I did. My mind floated to Henry, my little brother. He would be so proud to see where I had ended up, how I made it as I always said I would. My heart ached thinking of him and the little time that we were able to be together.

I was barely sixteen years old when he passed away at the age of ten. A drive by shooting on that very corner, we used to sell papers on, took him from me. Our mother had died long before that, drunk herself to death, leaving us with our grandparents who were much older, and I cared for them and Henry as best I could. After Henry died, I moved in with Barry. My grandparents passed when their house caught on fire about four months later and I was deemed legally the states problem. Lucky for me, Barry's parents stepped in and offered to foster me until I was of age, and the state allowed it, so I was able to continue working with him to build everything Nitrous Ruin was today.

I broke from the memory and pulled my gaze away from the suit. I walked back over to the bed where I had left my phone, I had about forty minutes to get my ass together and get downstairs. This was my big moment; I shouldn't squander it on memories of a past that I can't change. I tossed the phone back down, grabbed the suit from its hanger and headed into the bathroom.

CHAPTER 15

Lisey

"You're meeting him tonight after the dinner?"

"Should I change?"

"Absolutely, not." Aggie was fawning over the cobalt blue, knee-length cocktail dress I had chosen for the evenings attire.

"Don't you think it might be too much?"

"No. You look amazing." I smiled at her as she was clapping her hands together through the video call.

"Thank you."

"Girl." She said. I snapped my eyes up to the camera and she rolled her eyes at me. "Lose the glasses." I reached up and took them off, letting the loose curls held back by them fall, framing my face.

"Better?" I asked.

"There's my sexy bitch." I felt my cheeks turn red as she danced on the screen, swaying her hands from side to side.

"I don't want him to think me prude."

"If he does, then fuck him. You are in Scotland, baby. There isn't anything you can't handle. You might be there for work, but why not have a little fun at the same time?" I nodded she was right, but I was far from ready to give my body to someone, especially someone that I had met on a plane. I looked at the time in the corner.

"Shit. Aggie, I have to go."

"Alright, text me and tell me everything later."

"I will."

"Love you."

"Love you too." I ended the call, turned my phone to silent, before stuffing it into the black clutch that I had packed in my suitcase.

As the elevator came to a stop in the grand foyer, the doors opened and there was an attendant waiting on the other side.

"Miss Hammond?" I nodded. "This way please." He began to walk through the foyer towards a set of closed doors.

As he opened them my jaw all but hit the floor. The grandeur of the room was more than I had ever imagined, there were people all over the place, butlers, handing out glasses of champagne, a bartender mixing spirits and others walking around with finger foods like sandwiches and caviar. I hadn't been to an event so grand since my mom had taken me to Milan. The crystal chandelier that hung at the center of the room seemed to float as though it were held up by magic.

Mesmerized by the lights and the people, my cheeks instantly turned red, when I stepped backwards, knocking into someone. I turned right away. Jafe was standing there a glass of champagne in his hand.

"Jafe, I am so incredibly sorry." He smiled and switched his glass to his other hand, shaking the one he had freed of the glass.

"No worries, Miss Hammond, accidents happen. Let us hope that this will be the extent of those as we prepare to start shooting." I nodded. He looked over my shoulder and a smile spread across his face. "Ah, Mr. Rose, please come here, I would like for you to meet someone.

I felt a presence behind me and turned, my eyes locking with familiar blue ones. His eyes grazed across my face with a sense of recognition, but at the moment it was evident he didn't recognize me at all. He held his hand out to me. I took it firmly.

"Miss Hammond." It was as soon as my last name came from Jafe's mouth that his relaxed expression changed. So, he did remember. "Mr. Rose, our lead male." The look on his face seemed to be more stunned than anything.

"It's nice to meet you, Mr. Rose."

"Quinn, please." I went to pull my hand from his, but his fingers tightened ever so slightly on mine, stopping me. My eyes locked with his once more and he was looking deep into mine as though he was searching for some sort of answer.

"I have good news and bad news, alike I'm afraid," Jafe said. Quinn released my hand, and we both looked at him.

"Mr. George Ludwig, sent a contract over this afternoon."

"As in the screenwriter?" I asked, my heart beginning to pound in my chest. I had only ever heard of him by name, and studied his work with Gerry, but never had seen the man in person.

"The very same." My mind began to bounce around.

"I'm sorry, Jafe, but I thought I was hired to be your lead screenwriter?" I felt Quinn's eyes lock on me, as a heat resonated on my skin.

"We still very much want you to be a part of the production, Miss Hammond, your resume proceeds itself. With that being said, you will be working with Mr. Ludwig, as needed, but during the down time, I have another task for you."

"Which is?" He looked at Quinn and put his hand on his shoulder.

"Mr. Rose's assistant has malaria; the poor girl went on safari and is now bedridden."

"So, Miss Hammond?" Quinn said as he traced his eyes back to me.

"Will double as your assistant," Jafe said. His words knocked all of the air out of my lungs. This wasn't the job that I had signed up for. How did I go from lead screenwriter to being a gopher for Quinn? I forced a smile; I needed this job and to work with Ludwig would be a great honor for me and Gerry.

"Thank you Jafe, for finding room for me on such a packed production team. I would be happy to assist, Mr. Ludwig and Mr. Rose on anything they might need during filming." Jafe seemed to breathe a sigh of relief.

"Great! I'm so glad to hear that, Gerry said you were a hard worker, and she highly recommended you. I'm sorry that things changed last minute, Miss Hammond."

"It's no problem, really." I kept the smile on my face, but on the inside I was frustrated. Gerry wasn't going to be happy to hear that I was demoted to assistant. Jafe smiled and then quickly scanned his eyes across the room, seeing others that he knew. He clapped us both on our shoulders.

"Have fun tonight. The real work begins in the morning." Before either of us could say anything he disappeared into the crowd. I could feel a heat in my eyes, tears were coming, and I would be damned to show emotion in this room full of strangers. I took a deep breath and smiled at Quinn.

"Excuse me." I strode off before he could say anything.

CHAPTER 16

Quinn

I walked into the lower ballroom where they were having the party. The suit clung to me in all of the right places, perfectly tailored as I had requested it. I fidgeted with my cufflinks as I walked up to one of the butlers and took a glass of champagne.

"Mr. Rose." I looked over the brim of the crystal flute as I heard my name called from across the room. Jafe was standing there, waving me over and in front of him, with her back turned to me, stood a stunning brunette. Her legs were long and toned, kissed by the sun. Her soft curls, cascading down her back in twisted tendrils. The cobalt blue dress she did was hugging every curve in all the right places, her ass being my main focal point.

I strode over, my head high and shoulders square, my eyes continuing to casually glaze over her. I felt my member stir in my pants and I had to think of something else, like Barry, running naked through a venue after too many Irish car bombs. The thought of Barry naked alone was enough to send my stomach turning and quiet down my bulging friend.

"Miss Hammond." My stomach twisted in knots as she turned and those familiar emerald, green eyes struck me right in the dick. The thought of her underneath me, staring up with those eyes as she bit her lip sliced through me, causing friction in my pants. I could just slightly hear Jafe talking, but his words weren't registering in my mind as I was unable to tear my thoughts away from taking this girl to my bed. What were the odds that we would be working the same project and staying in the same hotel?

"Mr. Rose's assistant has malaria; the poor girl went on safari and is now bedridden." My mind snapped to the conversation before me and my growing member throbbed as I shifted trying to hide him in the crease of my pants. My eyes looked from her to Jafe.

"So, Miss Hammond?" It came out slow, heavy as I tried to stifle the hefty breath that wallowed in the back of my throat.

"Will double as your assistant," Jafe said. My eyes flicked back to her and her eyes flashed with a sudden shock. I wasn't sure what her role on the production team was, but I knew from the look in her eye that she wasn't expecting that. She plastered a smile on her face and then the room was filled with the most beautiful sound as she began to speak. My eyes staring hard at her plump pouty lips as she spoke, her words going in one ear and out the other. As she stopped speaking, I watched as her top teeth just grazed her lower lip ever so slightly, forcing me to suppress a growl.

Before I could make sense of the situation, Jafe excused himself and walked away, before she took off towards the exit of the room. I stood dumb-founded for a moment as I tried to calm my throbbing member, before moving through the crowd with my dick harder than concrete.

I wanted to go after her, I saw she was upset which meant she would need comforting, which was one of my specialties. With a wicked smirk, I turned in the direction she had left in and began to slowly make my way after her.

As I walked into the foyer, she was nowhere to be seen. Walking down a vacant hallway just a ways, I could hear her sing song voice coming from around the corner.

"I don't know what happened," her voice exuded shock, with a touch of sadness. There was silence for a moment, and I moved in closer so I could hear who she was talking to.

"This wasn't part of the plan, Gerry." There was a sniffle in her voice, she was crying. At the sound of another man's name, a tinge of irritation rose in my chest.

"It's not what we were promised, but it's still a movie credit. You could learn so much from Ludwig, I'm actually half tempted to get on a plane and join you over there." The sound of a woman's voice coming through the phone instantly set me at ease.

"They want me to be Quinn Rose's assistant." The words came out with a hint of malice, and I felt a grin, rise in the corners of my mouth. She was interested and she knew it; she was just putting on a show for her boss.

"Lisey, you listen to me. Do not fall for that playboy's games. He has a reputation with women and it's not a good one." This woman was trying to sway my little minx.

"I understand, Gerry. I'm just here to do the job, learn what I can and get home."

"Try to have some fun while you are there."

"I will."

"Just stay safe and stay away from that rocker, man whore."

"Yes, Gerry." I felt a thrill of excitement shoot down my spine, she was going to play hard to get and currently I was only interested in this game we were playing. Normally, I wasn't one to bother, if a girl wasn't interested, then I would move on to the next, but this was one conquest, I was willing to go to desperate lengths to conquer.

Chapter 17

Lisey

I found a quiet place in the hallway and immediately pulled my phone from within my clutch. Dialing Gerry's number, I put the phone to my ear.

"Lisey, how's it going?"

"Terrible."

"What happened?" I felt the tears that I had shoved down beginning to run freely down my face in the solace of the empty hallway.

"Ludwig joined the production team. They said I could assist him as needed but was essentially no longer the head screenwriter."

"Ludwig? I had read that he had turned down that contract."

"Apparently, he changed his mind." I felt air getting caught in my throat as I spoke.

"Calm down, Lisey." Her voice was soft and calming. Gerry always had a funny way of getting me to calm down with the slightest sound of her voice. That's probably why she was the head of our team, she exuded calm, no matter the chaos that was unfolding.

"I don't know what happened."

"It's going to be okay, you're still there, if they didn't want to keep you then they would be sending you home, first thing tomorrow."

"This wasn't part of the plan, Gerry." I sniffled as my nose began to clog.

"It's not what we were promised, but it's still a movie credit. You could learn so much from Ludwig, I'm actually half tempted to get on a plane and join you over there." I laughed slightly at the thought of her rolling in here, ready to meet a man so legendary that none of us had ever worked with him in person, he only worked with the best. This film was promising for academy awards, based on the book by Charlotte Pague. The other part of the conversation rose to the front of my mind, and I scoffed slightly.

"They want me to be Quinn Rose's assistant." There was silence briefly on the other end of the phone.

"Lisey, you listen to me. Do not fall for that playboy's games. He has a reputation with women and it's not a good one." Her tone was low and serious.

I had no idea who this man even was when I met him on the plane. Last night he was simply Q. Now he was the rockstar seducer that Aggie had told me about. She was going to flip her lid when I told her that it was him that I had met on the plane. My mind went back to those moments, the way he looked at me, the way he touched me, and I felt a heat coil in my stomach, radiating downward, I shifted uncomfortably against the wall. Forcing the tingling desire away from between my thighs and out of my body.

"I understand, Gerry. I'm just here to do the job, learn what I can and get home."

"Try to have some fun while you are there."

"I will."

"Just stay safe and stay away from that rocker, man whore."

"Yes, Gerry."

"Give me a call tomorrow when you get done for the day, I want to hear about everything."

"I will."

"Goodnight, Lisey."

"Goodnight." The call ended and I turned, running face first into the firm chest of my new boss. I held my hands up as I stepped back.

"Mr. Rose, I'm sorry, I didn't see you there." I felt the dampness of the remaining tears on my face and quickly dashed them away with my hand.

"It's Q," he said quietly, a low growl emanating from his throat. I felt my legs shake briefly and I braced myself against the wall casually. He leaned int, placing his hand against the wall. "Are you okay?" There was something hidden in his question that I recognized, right away. The sound of seduction. I pushed off the wall forcing him back as I put distance between us.

"I'm fine, Mr. Rose. Thank you for your concern." I stuffed my phone back into my clutch with agitation and stormed off, leaving him alone in the hallway.

Re-entering the party, I found a butler with champagne and gracefully took a glass, before gliding to the bar. Standing there, I downed it in two gulps, before setting it down as the handsome bartender, eyed me.

"Need something a little stronger?" he asked. His brown eyes locking with mine. I sighed heavily.

"Yes, please."

"What will it be?"

"A whiskey and could you please make it a double?"

"Rocks or straight?"

"Straight." He cocked his eyebrow at me and flashed me a sideways smile as he turned to get the drink for me.

When he turned back he gently slid the rocks glass towards me and then leaned on the bar, towards me.

"Rought night?"

"You have no idea." I took the glass and threw back the double, like it was nothing, the fire, heating my throat as it slid down smoothly.

"What happened?" I put the glass down on the bar as he eyes me curiously. A few more of these and I was bound to tell this stranger my entire life story.

"A lot."

"Would you like another?" he asked as he eyed the glass on the table.

"Please." He nodded, knocking on the bar twice.

"Coming right up, my lady." Heat flashed in my cheeks as he turned his back to me, my eyes trailing to his exquisite ass as the pants he wore shaped it nicely. Lisey. I scolded myself, a small smile creasing into the corner of my mouth as I turned my eyes to glance around the room, looking for Q.

The sound of the glass being replaced on the bar grabbed my attention and I turned, taking it once more in my hand, fingering the rim with my index finger.

"So, which one of these pompous assholes broke you heart, love?"

"The one that hired me." He leaned on the bar again, curiosity exuding through his eyes as they locked with mine.

"Don't let him get you down." I smiled slightly as I raised the glass and again downed another double. I set the glass down and used my thumb to wipe away a little bit that had slipped down the rim onto my lip.

"Here." He reached out, my body tense as his hand came across the bar. Suddenly, my eyes went wide with horror as a hand shot out from the corner of my vision, just as his thumb graced my bottom lip. I turned to see Q, his eyes radiating a fire that I could feel in my soul.

CHAPTER 18

Quinn

As I walked back into the room, joining the rest of the crew and production team, I glanced around the room. Spotting Lisey, standing at the bar as the bartender was reaching out to touch her.

A fire ignited inside of me.

I couldn't explain it.

I barely knew her, but the claim...

It was already there.

I strode over, quickly grabbing his wrist and yanking his hand away.

"Don't touch her," I growled. His eyes locked with mine and the disgust within them was evident.

"Mr. Rose?" she said exasperated. The bartender yanked his arm away.

"Chill out man."

"Don't tell me to chill out," I hissed. I felt something soft on my arm and shifted my gaze, peering into those green eyes as they exuded fear. I glanced around the room and there were several people watching the spectacle.

"Quinn, stop." Lisey whispered. My eyes snapped back to her, and I had to stop every urge in my body to cup her face and pull her in for a deep kiss.

"Marina, everyone." Jafe's voice boomed throughout the room and gasps rose into the air as they all turned toward the door. My eyes followed. Walking into the room, was the tall, raven haired, beauty that led the band Diocese. Roddy had been trying to get with their team for a while now, to get us on a tour together.

"Wow." It came out in a long breath. She was even more stunning in person. Instead of adorning her usual stage wear, she was wearing a floor length gown of black satin. The draped neckline accentuating her cleavage, I felt a twitch in my groin but nothing more. Just a small wisp of excitement that faded quickly. I felt the gentle fingers that had wrapped around my arm disappear. Returning my gaze, I caught a glimpse of Lisey as she disappeared through the crowd, towards the exit.

I turned back toward the bartender in a huff. He stood eyeing me with disdain, as though I had just ruined the ending of his favorite show. I leaned against the bar, keeping my voice low.

"If I ever see you so much as look in her direction again, I'll." I stopped. I couldn't verbally threaten this man in front of half the production team. His demeanor remained the same, unphased. I flexed my hand, the tattoo of the snake bright in the light. A smirk spread to the corner of my mouth as the idea to lay him out cold on the floor came across my mind. There were too many people around and it was the first time I was meeting most of them. I didn't want to lose this gig.

I leaned across the bar top. My arms crossed under my chest to keep them from swinging.

As though I was ordering a drink.

"Keep your hands to yourself and I'll let you keep them," my tone low, the promise lingered in the words. He seemed taken aback by my response and his shoulders fell slightly. I knocked on the bar twice with a smile, before pushing off and heading into the crowd to meet my co-star.

Jafe grabbed me almost immediately and pushed me to the front of the crowd.

"Marina, this is Quinn, your co-star." She had her back turned, as she spoke to another member of production. She turned, holding out her hand. I took it gracefully and gently pulled it to my lips, planting a soft kiss. Her skin was like cashmere and smelled of vanilla.

"It's a pleasure to meet you," I said. She smiled as she gently took her hand back.

"Quinn Rose, I have heard of you. My manager says your team has been trying to contact us to set up a tour." My heart leapt into my throat. I hadn't felt something like this since the day we signed with CutThroat Records.

"We have, I understand that it can be hard with schedules and recording time."

"That it is. If this movie goes well then we can talk about it after."

"That would be great." She reached up and ran her thumb along my cheek, sending a shiver down my spine. I held my composure; I wasn't a ninny.

"I look forward to working with you."

"As I do." She smiled and let her hand fall, before disappearing into the crowd as Jafe gently took her by the arm and led her off to meet other people.

Lisey. My mind wandered back to that moment at the bar. Normally, I would have laid that guy out and asked questions later, but her voice, the way she gripped my arm gently, had stopped me. I looked around the room and in the crowd, I couldn't see her.

I made my way to the front desk, where a gentleman in a suit was standing in front of the computer.

"How can I help you?" he asked.

"I need the room number for Miss Hammond." He began tapping away on his computer. It wasn't exceedingly long before he looked up at me.

"Miss Hammond is staying in room six-thir-ty-five." She was right next door to me. I nodded my head and turned, walking toward the elevator.

When the lift stopped, I got off and walked straight to her room. Passing my room, my arm reached out, and I was knocking without a second thought. I wanted to check on her, the fear she held in her eyes during the encounter at the bar, flashing before my eyes.

There was no answer.

"Lisey?" I called. Again, there was no answer. I knocked again and once more she didn't come to the door. I waited for a moment to see if she would show up if she believed that I was gone, but she never came to the door.

I stuffed my hands in my pockets and walked away, back towards the elevator.

Downstairs, I peered into the ballroom, they were getting ready to serve dinner and as the lead, I suppose I was expected to be there. I looked at my phone; I had a few minutes. I opened my messages texting her quickly.

'Where did you go? The dinner is starting.'

I stuffed my phone back into my pocket and headed in.

Everyone was taking their seats. I stood in the doorway, looking for an open seat when Jafe waved to me from the far end. I made my way over to him as Marina stood at his side.

"I thought it would be nice for you two to get better acquainted as you will be working closely together for the next several months." I nodded and he sauntered off to seat others. I placed my hands on the high-backed chair and pulled it out gently for her. Her baby blue eyes locked with mine as a small smile creased in the corner of her lip. She took her seat.

"Thank you," she said her voice sultry as it entered my ears. Again, I was surprised that there wasn't more going on in my pants as my eyes were cast upon this beauty. I smiled and took my seat at her side.

Under the table, I pulled my phone from my pocket, looking to see if Lisey had yet replied. To my dismay there was no response.

CHAPTER 19

Lisey

"I can't believe you are working with Quinn Rose!" Aggie squealed.

"Yeah, his assistant." I flopped back on my bed, the phone in my hand as she stared at me through the screen.

"At least they are still keeping you on the project and that Lucas guy is all you ever talk about."

"Ludwig. I know. It's amazing that I have the opportunity to work with him, but still I can't help but feel like I did something wrong."

"You didn't do anything wrong." I put my hand on my forehead and sighed heavily.

"You should have seen the way he reacted to that bartender, Aggie."

"Was it hot?" I rolled my eyes at her through the camera. It was kind of hot to see him that way, the way his chest puffed behind his specially tailored suit, his eyes expressing something that I couldn't quite discern between jealousy and anger.

"It was weird."

"He was probably just being protective of you."

"I'm just his assistant Aggie."

"Well, who knows, maybe he has a thing for assistants."

"Gerry, told me he was a man whore, a bad reputation with woman."

"He definitely has a reputation, but God, look at the man. He's hot as fuck." I heard the chime from the elevator echo in the distance.

"Hold on for a second." I muted the speaker and quietly waited.

I practically jumped six feet in the air as a knock, broke the quiet that had fallen, stiffening me. I remained frozen in place, unable to move.

"Lisey?" His voice crept through from under the door. I had about enough of Quinn Rose for today. From finding out that he was the lead that I was practically drooling over on the plane when he was just another traveler. My cheeks flushed with embarrassment as I thought back to the flight. The way he cupped my face and kissed me on the forehead, the way I had just sat there and let him do it.

The knocking came a second time, and I stood, padding gently over to the door and peeking through the hole. He was standing there, waiting. I watched him step off to the side and lean against the wall for a moment as though I would emerge, if I believed he had walked away. I had dealt with enough paparazzi traveling with my mother to know that old goose trick.

Moments later, he stuffed his hands in his pockets and began walking away.

It wasn't until I heard the ding of the elevator as it arrived back on the floor that I returned to my video call with Aggie.

"What happened?" she asked.

"He came to my room."

"You didn't answer?"

"No."

"Why not?"

"Too much has happened. I just need some time to myself."

"Aren't you supposed to be at a dinner?"

"I don't feel well." She cocked her eyebrow at me. She knew that I was full of shit.

"What are you going to do then?"

"I think I might pop out to a real bar."

"Sounds like a plan to me."

"I'm going to wait a little bit until the dinner starts, so that way they will be distracted and won't see me leave."

"Sneaky, sneaky," Aggie chided. A notification popped up on my phone then, a message from Q. I read part of it before it disappeared and decided it would be best to leave it lie.

"What is it?" Aggie asked.

"He texted, wanted to know where I was, that the dinner was starting."

"He must want you there."

"Yeah, well I need to think about stuff. All in twenty-four hours, I met a handsome man on a plane and then became his personal assistant while simultaneously losing my original position all at once." Aggie sighed as she rested her head on her hand.

"Go get a drink and for the love of all creation, get some dick. It will make you feel better." I felt my cheeks go red.

"I'm going to change."

"No, ma'am, you leave the librarian on the floor where she is currently, and you go out there and have fun. You are Ellisia Hammond, the daughter of the world-renowned Elenor Fitz, go let your hair down and shake that fine ass of yours."

"I'm trying to escape her shadow, Aggie, not live in it."

"Does it really matter tonight? Last time I checked there are no shadows when the sun goes down." I grimaced at her through the phone, and she rolled her eyes at me.

"Go. Get ready." I glanced at the armoire in my room and then gave her the side eye.

"What should I wear?"

"Well either what you are wearing now, because that ass though, or you could change if you really wanted to." I looked down at the dress I was wearing, it seemed a little fancy and would probably draw too much attention in a pub.

"Let me get changed really quick."

"No librarian."

"I'll let you decide." I left the phone facing up on the bed as I walked over and began sifting through the clothes that I had hung up earlier.

When I picked up the phone again, I was wearing a black crop top, with skinny jeans.

"Turn around." I turned all the way around.

"Do it again, but stay facing away from me," Aggie said. I turned a one eighty and then stood facing away from the camera.

"Hop."

"What?"

"I said hop." I did a little bunny hop and felt the tightness of the jeans stretch across my ass as it jiggled.

"That's what I'm talking about, look at that ass." I laughed as I turned around.

"This work?" I asked.

"The cut of that top is hot as hell too." She put her hand to her lips, blowing a chef's kiss. "Bellissima." I looked at the time on the clock, that sat on the nightstand.

"It's probably been long enough that I can go."

"Get out there and get the three S's."

"Three S's."

"Shots, shaft and sleep."

"Aggie."

"Don't argue, get out there." I laughed slightly as I ran my free hand through my hair.

"I'll call you tomorrow."

"Love you, bestie."

"Love you too." The call ended and I got up from the bed. Walking to the door, I slipped into my jacket and then made my way downstairs.

As the elevator stopped at the bottom, I peered into the grand foyer before fully exiting. There was no one around. I could hear the faint squabble of voices coming from down the hallway, where I assumed that the dinner was taking place. Breathing a sigh of relief, I slipped my hands into my pockets and causally made my way to the door.

As I walked out onto the street, I remembered that Quinn had said something about a bar nearby. I pulled my phone free from my back pocket and found the address. Launching the directions, I made my way down the street.

Chapter 20

Quinn

As the dinner lagged on, my mind kept going to the phone in my pocket as it remained silent. Lisey hadn't responded to my text and as far as I knew she hadn't even read it yet. Part of me wanted to get up and walk away, to find her and if not her then a stiff drink and possibly some dessert.

"Where is Miss Hammond?" Jafe asked me from across the table. I looked around as eyes were on me.

"Miss Hammond was rather tired from her journey and asked if she could be excused." Jafe nodded satiated.

"That was nice of you to give her the night off," Marina said at my side.

"She's going to be busy for the next several months, she should rest. I know she had a long flight."

"Well, I look forward to getting to work with both of you." I nodded.

"Have you met your assistant yet?" She nodded and looked down the table a ways. A young man with slicked back blonde hair, nodded in her direction.

"His name is Davi, his from Hungary."

"He seems like a nice fellow."

"So far he speaks very limited English, but that's okay, he is fluent in French as am I."

"I didn't know you could speak French."

"One of my many talents." Her crimson lips spread, releasing a brilliant smile.

Finally, when the dinner was over, I quickly made my way back up to my room. Stopping once more at Lisey's door. I knocked.

No response.

"Lisey, if you are in there could you come out and talk to me please?" I waited and was still met with silence. I heard people coming around the corner. As they saw me standing outside the door, they eyeballed me slightly. I smiled at them and waved. They continued past me, and I went to my room.

I pulled my phone from my pocket and tossed it on to the bed.

I removed my suit and threw it back on the hanger that I had retrieved it from. Hanging it back up in the armoire; I would have it sent out for dry cleaning in the morning. I pulled a pair of jeans from the dresser and put them on, before grabbing a black button-down shirt. Tossing it over my shoulders, I left it open, exposing the gray beater I was wearing underneath.

I picked my phone up off the bed and looked at it again to see if there was anything from her and was met with disappointment. Grumbling, I shoved it into my back pocket and headed toward the door.

As I walked out of the hotel and on to the street, the cool night air hit me. The smell of the crisp air was a welcome scent after living in the smoggy city of LA. The air was never nearly this clean back home. I inhaled deeply, letting it calm me.

Walking down the sidewalk toward the nearest bar, I noticed traffic was busier than I had anticipated.

Entering the Black Bull Tavern, the music was loud and there were men hooting and hollering near the bar. I walked over to see what all the commotion was about, when I saw her standing on the counter, throwing back an amber brown liquid from a shot glass.

"Lisey?" Her name left my lips as a whisper. I moved closer, trying to push myself through the throng of men to get to her.

"Another, please," she said in a pouty tone. I could tell from the way she was acting that she was completely hammered. The bartender held up a bottle and filled the shot glass once more. She tossed it back, her brown curls shaking freely as she moved around, stumbling on the bar top. A sudden desperation propelled me forward and I reached the edge of the bar, just as she spun, her foot catching the side sending her falling backwards.

I held my arms out and she fell into them, now cradled against my chest. I looked into her eyes. They were glazed over; she was drunk as fuck.

"Lisey, I." She cupped my face with her hand and pushed her lips to mine, forceful, hungry, filled with desire.

She was drunk and clinging to me like I was the last steady thing in the room.

The fire that shot through my body went straight to my groin, my dick hardening. I pushed back against her, tasting the whiskey on her lips briefly before I pushed my tongue into her mouth.

Her fingers tightened against my face and the patrons at the bar seemed to be cheering us on. They were enjoying the show. I began to pull away from her, biting her lip ever so slightly, a moan escaping her lips. I leaned my forehead against hers as her chest heaved. It was then I realized that mine was always heaving, the heat and the excitement still radiating through us as I stood there, still cradling her in my arms.

"Are you going to put me down?" She asked with a pout. I lifted my head slightly and kissed her forehead, for some reason I didn't want to, but I couldn't hold her like this all night.

"Yeah," I replied with a breathy sigh. I set her back down on her feet and she wobbled dangerously. I took her back in my arms, and she leaned against me, her swimming green eyes staring up at me through her full thick lashes.

"We should get you back to the hotel." She pushed off me like I had offended her somehow.

"No, I'm having fun." She turned back to the group of gentlemen as they began to feed her shots once more. One man tried to push one into her hand and I took it from him and set it on the bar. I gently took her shoulders and pulled her away from the group of men.

"What are you doing?" she asked.

"Getting you some air." We stepped out of the bar and on to the sidewalk.

"I don't need air."

"Yes, you do."

"You know you aren't technically able to boss me around until tomorrow."

"I'm not bossing you around. I'm trying to take care of you."

"I can take care of myself." Her words slurred, tone defiant.

"Just humor me." She looked at me. She huffed and then wrapped her arms tightly around herself before she sat down on the curb. I took a seat next to her.

"I'm not ready to go back."

"That's fine, we can stay. You just might want to slow down a bit."

"Why?" I pulled my phone from my pocket.

"It's only nine-fifteen."

"Looks like I made it on time for our date then," she laughed. She leaned over and rested her head against my shoulder. I was surprised she remembered. I thought that after what had transpired earlier at the cocktail party, that she would have run straight for the hills.

"Yeah, you are. I was a little late, I hope you can forgive me."

"Just this time," she said. Her curls shifted against my bare arm, and I felt a tingle radiate up my spine.

After a little while she jumped to her feet, practically stumbling towards the door. I reached it before she did, holding it open for her. She nodded at me, gave me a half-cocked salute, and then walked inside.

As we walked in, the group of men that had once crowded the bar were now sitting, scattered around at separate tables, the music now returned to a softer volume. I heaved a silent breath of relief as we approached the bar as none of them seemed to be paying any attention. I found us two open seats at the bar, and we took a seat. The bartender approached.

"What can I get you folks?" He looked at her with recognition. "Would you like another whiskey, love?" I placed my hand over hers and the bartenders eyes drifted to me.

"I think we will have two beers please." The bartender nodded and turned to get the beverages.

"I don't remember the last time I actually had a beer," Lisey said beside me.

"Well, I'm more of a liquor man myself, but I think we need a little break from that, what do you think?"

"You're in charge, boss." A hint of sarcasm behind her words. The bartender turned, leaving two foaming pints on the bar. I reached towards them and pulled them closer, putting one in front of her.

"Thank you." I nodded and the bartender caught my eye.

"What's her bill?" I asked. He turned to the cash register behind him.

When he turned back he held his hands up.

"She doesn't have a tab; she hasn't paid for a single drink all night." My eyes drifted to her, catching the staggering cut of her cut off shirt, the curve of her breasts visible. No wonder she hadn't paid for anything, these guys were like a pack of dogs, and she was the bone.

I couldn't remember how long it had been, but there were several empty shot and pint glasses spread before us. My head swimming as the alcohol buzzed through my body. My eyes traced to Lisey as she was finishing the last of the pint in her hand. She was still fully alert and whatever she was feeling when I had gotten here seemed to dissipate. Her tolerance was incredible. She placed the empty glass on the bar and leaned into me, her hand rubbing my thigh. I looked down at her, and she raised her eyes, through her lashes.

"Let's go back." I downed the rest of my beer.

"Alright." Putting the glass down, I acknowledged the bartender. "Check please." He nodded.

We stumbled into the lobby and towards the elevator. The man at the front desk nodding at us as we made our way through. The hallways now quieter than they had been earlier as the giant clock on the wall, chimed the eleventh hour.

On our floor, I walked her to her room, and she turned, leaning against the door.

"What?" I whispered. She pushed herself forward, and her lips crashed into mine. Her hands in my hair, tugging on it as a low growl emanated from my chest into her mouth. A slight moan escaped her, and I picked her up. She wrapped her legs around me and I turned. Using the wall to hold her up, I fished the key from my pocket and unlocked my door. Pushing it open, I carried her inside.

Chapter 21

Lisey

As I walked into the bar, there was the lingering smell of cigar smoke. I was so used to the bars not allowing smoking that I was caught off guard.

Approaching the counter, the bartender turned to me as he was wiping down a glass with a rag, he smiled slightly.

"What can I get ye, wee darling?" His Scottish accent thick.

"I'll have a whiskey please, dealer's choice."

"Double or single?"

"Double please." He nodded and turned to get my drink ready.

He turned back to me and set the shot on the bar. I reached for it.

"Would ye like a slate lassie?" I reached for my card, that was housed in my back pocket, in the corner of my eye, I saw a figure approach my right side.

"Put it on my tab, Owen." The bartender nodded and turned away. I looked at the man, he was older, no more than thirty maybe.

"I recognize you," he said quietly. I felt a chill go up my spine.

"Oh, you do?" I asked casually.

"Aye, you look just like your mother." I turned to him, my heart racing. I had come across men who were crazy about my mother before, some were dangerous.

"Are you a fan of hers?" I asked softly, trying to hide the tremble in my voice.

"Not in the way you think." His eyes locked with mine and it was then that there was something familiar about them. "She is after all my dear, Auntie. Despite how things ended with yer parents, I still love her dearly, cousin." My heart all but stopped.

"Archibold?" He smiled.

"Aye, I didn't think ye'd would recognize me, cousin. It's been too long." I turned to him, and he enveloped me in a tight embrace.

"It's so good to see you. My dad said that he had told you that I was going to be here." He pulled away.

"Aye, I was planning to call on ye tomorrow, to see if ye'd grab a bite with me. Dinnae expect to find ye here."

"What do you mean by that?" I asked as I scrunched my nose at him.

"This place is midden."

"Oi, you don't like it, ye can leave," Owen said.

"Haud yer wheesht," Archibold said with a smile. He cocked his head towards Owen. "We're auld freends, he's a braw lad." I smiled, nodded, and then picked up my glass and threw back the double. As I tipped my head forward again and set the glass down, Archibold looked at me like he was seeing a ghost.

"What?"

"The States disnae agree with you, cousin." He turned his attention to Owen.

"Git the lass another yin."

"Aye."

"Pit her swallie on ma slate." I turned to him.

"Archibold."

"Archie, cousin." He said with a smirk.

"I can get my own drinks really."

"Dinnae fash." Owen appeared with another glass. Archie looked at Owen. "This is my wee cousin from The States, she's here working on a huge project." I grabbed his arm, no one was supposed to know about it.

"Aye, what is it then?" Owen asked.

"A piece on Highlander Architecture," I blurted. Archie looked at me and cocked an eyebrow. I looked at him and shook my head subtly.

"Ye learn a lot in the highlands. But yer a wee bit far from them." Owen said.

"I'll be here for a while, traveling for research."

"Aye, well haste ye back." I looked back at him and smiled with a nod. It was then he walked away, tending another customer who had just arrived at the bar.

"What was that all about?"

"No one is supposed to know about the movie." My voice was quiet, almost a whisper.

"Yer pa told me about it."

"He wasn't supposed to." He gently patted my hand, which was still gently gripping his arm.

"No fear, dear cousin, I'll tell not a soul." I nodded and released his arm, surprised I was still holding it.

We had several drinks before he got up to leave.

"Would you like me to take you back to your hotel? The streets of Edinburgh can get rowdy at night."

"I'll be okay, I'm just a block away."

"Are ye sure?" I nodded. He leaned over and kissed me gently on the cheek.

"I'll see you soon." I said.

"Yes, you must come to the house and meet the family, Claire will be happy to meet you and the children as well."

"I look forward to meeting them." He nodded and then disappeared through the door.

I turned my attention back to the drink in front of me. Then something happened. A song came on in the background that moved through my soul, forcing me to stand and move around on the floor. Others who were sitting around, watching the highlights from the latest futbol game, turned their attention to me.

I don't know how it happened, but before I knew it I was on the bar, dancing to this song, telling the bartender to play it again. The men who had been sitting around the room approached.

"What's she having? I'll buy."

"The lass needs another yin."

"Let yer hair down lassie." Their words began to muddle together as I danced around, oblivious to the precariousness of my situation. The music loud, my thoughts free from the burdens that exhausted me.

As my shot glass ran dry, I tipped back.

"Another, please?" My voice was pouty, with a sultry divinity to it. Owen grabbed the bottle he had been keeping close at hand and filled the glass again. Standing straight up, I threw it back. Moving around some more when suddenly my foot caught something, and I felt myself flailing backwards.

I fell, waiting for the solid surface of the earth to grasp me when I suddenly stopped, strong arms cradling me. I looked up and my eyes went wide, despite the swimming in my head.

Quinn.

Shit.

"Lisey." His voice held a desperation, and my fingers found his cheek, a hint of stubble scratching them as I pulled him to me, pushing my lips on to his. It seemed wrong but at the same time it felt so right. He growled slightly, before pushing his tongue into my mouth.

The next thing I knew, we were standing outside of my room. I leaned against the door, using it to support me as I was too tired and drunk to hold myself up. My eyes locked with him and this needing fire radiated through my body. I wanted him. I wanted him to take me as his own.

"What?" The questions cool coming from his lips. I pushed myself from the door and into him, kissing him. Heat, passion, desire, pulsing through me, he picked me up, making my stomach coil, sending the radiance down between my thighs, throbbing, desperate to feel a touch that I'd never felt, to be taken. He leans me against the wall, fishing for the key in his pocket.

As he unlocked the door, my breath hitched as he once again locked his lips with mine, carrying me into the room.

He kicked the door closed behind us as he walked over towards the bed, dipping me low to lay me on the soft comforter. The satiny texture sent chills through every fiber of my being as he continued to kiss me. His hands reached for my shirt, drifting it up and over my head, exposing my bare breasts to him. His hands moved over them, caressing them, kneading them gently.

It was when he pinched my nipple that a moan loudly escaped me. He sat back, pulling his mouth away from mine, his smile gleaming in the darkness.

He began to kiss my neck, sucking and licking as he trailed down, over my collar bone, between my breasts and then finally settling on the right one. Flicking, sucking, biting, his mouth assaulting one as the his other hand desperately kneaded the other. I felt the pressure building inside of me to scream out as the new feelings radiated through every nerve.

I bit my lower lip as I let my body take over naturally.

Allowing my back to arch upwards, pushing my chest upwards.

The movements of his hand became quickened, more desperate, more needing.

It was then that I felt his hand leave my breast and begin to trail down the front of my stomach, over my naval and towards the top of my jeans. A shiver of pleasure raced through my body as I felt goosebumps rising on my skin. My hips arched upward, and he snickered playfully.

His hand slipped under the tight waist of my jeans, sliding over my panties. He pushed down with his fingers as they slid into the fold, immediately finding my clit. He stopped, pulled his mouth away from my breast, panting as he looked at me.

"You've soaked through your panties," he mused. I opened my mouth to respond, but he put more pressure on my clit, circling through my panties that forced me to suck back a sharp breath. Replacing whatever I was going to say with a moan. My hips rose up to meet his hand. He smiled and pulled his hand from inside, immediately unbuttoning and then swiftly removing them. Leaving me bare, my panties exposed.

"Let's just remove these," he said softly. I laid there, entranced, as he slowly took them off. He tossed them to the side and looked at me. I felt a flush of embarrassment flood my face, no one had ever seen me completely bare.

"You're beautiful," he said. I suddenly felt his hand rubbing over me, his palm dealing a pressure that sent a wave of pleasure through me as it slid up and down my mound. His thumb found my clit and began to circle it, first slowly and then quickening, forcing me to arch my back and buck my hips. A pressure building inside of me that made me want to scream out.

"Come for me," he growled lowly. He quickened his pace. My breath short in between moans, trying to keep quiet, to keep from screaming out.

"Come for me. Or else," he threatened. I bit my lip and sucked in a huge breath.

"Or else what?" His hand immediately stopped. He pushed my legs apart and dipped his head down low. A loud moan began to force its way to my lips when I felt a hand over my mouth. There was a dampness to it, and I could smell my arousal on his hand. My hips bucked upwards as his tongue devoured me, every flick, every suckle, sent my body reeling as repeated waves of pleasure rocked through me.

He removed his hand, standing up seemingly satisfied, staring down at me. My chest heaved as my body continued to shake as the residual waves dissipated. He crawled back up to me, his lips meeting mine once again, as his hand trailed between my folds, making me pant and shake further. He kissed me hard before pulling away. Dropping his pants to the floor, his member, hard as fuck. He got down between my legs, kneeling, with his cock ready in hand. I felt him moving the tip, between my folds wetting himself.

And then..

I. Fucking. Panicked.

"Stop!"

CHAPTER 22

Quinn

I instantly threw myself back off the bed, slamming against the armoire. My chest heaving as my cock throbbed. She scrambled, pulling her legs in tight to her chest. That was it.

"I'm sorry." Her words were filled with something that I couldn't quite name. She jumped out of the bed and quickly grabbed her clothes. Rushing out the door before I could even say anything.

I walked over and turned the light on, so I could find my own pants.

Grabbing them from the floor, I silently curse myself. What the fuck was I thinking? We had been out drinking, heavily and to let her have one small act of passion that consumed me, bringing her in here. We were so close. Close to feeding this ache that radiated through my body, the desire to have her.

I felt my cock suppress and looked down. She had said stop and that was the magic word for me. Stop meant, no more chasing, no more wanting. She wasn't the first girl that it happened with, and I was sure she wouldn't be the last. I put my pants on and looked at the door where she had disappeared through. I walked over and put the latch on.

As I got into bed, I could feel the wetness from her juices as she had come repeatedly. This would be the first, last and only time I would ever have her in my bed. Everything needed to stop. I laced my fingers and rested my head on my hands, staring at the ceiling.

Tomorrow things will have to go on the way they were meant to be.

I had to keep her away from me.

At all cost.

Even if it meant making her hate me.

***

The next morning, there was a knock at the door. I rolled over and looked at my phone; it was five in the morning. Groaning, I got up and walked over. As I cracked it open, I could clearly see Lisey's face on the other side. I pulled it all the way open and leaned in the doorframe.

"What do you want?" I asked heated. I didn't like to be woken up.

"I'm sorry, Mr. Rose, the other cast members are ready for the reading, and they asked me to retrieve you." She averted her eyes, unable to bring herself to look at me.

"Do you have my coffee?" I sighed as I rubbed the bridge of my nose.

"I didn't know you wanted coffee, but I can go get you some, if you just let me know what you'd like." I looked at her, and her eyes were still on the floor, as she reached in her pocket and pulled out a pad of paper.

"Coffee, black."

"Is that all?" I cocked a sideways smile and nodded.

My eyes moved to her lips.

Knock it off Q!

With one quick motion, I slammed the door in her face. I dusted my hands off and walked to the armoire to get ready for the reading.

I arrived downstairs in sweatpants and a hoodie, it was chilly this morning and with it being a reading, I didn't care how I showed up. Jafe rushed towards me as I entered the room.

"Mr. Rose, good morning, how is your room? Is everything to your liking?" I looked at the table in the room. Marina was sitting along the long side, with a seat open for me, as a few others were sitting around her.

"Yes, everything is great." I peered around the room and saw Lisey, standing, her back to the wall behind where my chair was placed at the table. I walked over and took my seat.

As I got comfortable she approached me and placed the cup of coffee on the table in front of me. I picked it up and took a sip. It was vile and I hated black coffee; it was also cold. I saw her retreat to the wall in my peripheral. I waited until she turned against the wall to call her back.

"Miss Hammond." She approached my right side quickly.

Her eyes cast down.

She wouldn't even look at me.

A breath hitched in my chest.

"Yes, Mr. Rose."

"This coffee is cold," I said with a stern quiet. She quickly took the cup and disappeared towards a table in the corner. I leaned over to Marina. "Sorry, to have kept you all waiting."

"No worries, the director isn't quiet here yet." There was a fellow sitting next to her that leaned over and held out his hand.

"Hi, I didn't get to meet you yesterday. I'm Branigan, your opposite in the movie. You can call me Bran." I took his hand and shook it.

"Quinn Rose, you can call me Q." It was then that I heard the light padding of her footsteps coming across the room that I turned as she handed me a fresh cup of coffee. I didn't acknowledge her as I took it.

We were all quietly talking when the room suddenly went dead silent. Turning my head, a tall, salty haired man walked in, his glasses sitting high on the bridge of his nose. He walked along the opposite side of the table and eyed us closely.

"Director Hardy, this is your cast," Jafe said. I watched as Hardy nodded his head as he eyed us over.

"Who is she?" he asked, pointing in our direction.

"Marina, your lea."

"Not her. The girl in the back, by the wall," Hardy interrupted.

"Mr. Rose's assistant."

"I thought his assistant was out with malaria?"

"We found a new one, Miss Hammond."

"Ah, yes, Miss Hammond, the woman we hired for screenwriting."

"Yes, Mr. Hardy." I watched as he walked around the table, turning in my chair to keep an eye on him as he approached Lisey. He took her hand and held it in his briefly, looking into her eyes.

"I'm sorry for the mix up my dear, I will personally send a letter to Gerry about the mishap. Also, I'm a huge fan of your mother, I am honored to have her daughter here working with us, no matter what capacity." His words struck something inside of me. Her mother? Who the hell was Lisey's mother? Why would he be a fan? I pushed the thoughts away and watched as Lisey's face went red and she nodded her head.

"Thank you, Mr. Hardy," she said quietly.

"My dear, you can call me Mage, all my friends do," he said with a wink.

"Thank you, Mage." He smiled and nodded, shaking her hand once more before turning back to the rest of us at the table.

"Does everyone have their script in front of them?" I looked down at the table, staring at the thick booklet in front of me.

"Yes, Mr. Hardy, everyone has a script and are ready to start when you are, sir." Hardy nodded as he walked over to a seat opposite Bran, Marina, and me. He took a seat and opened his own booklet.

"Let's start from the beginning."

It was noon before we left the room. Hardy wanted us to go for lunch and then come back for more reading. We had read through the first twelve scenes. I was amped to get to set and start working on the actual filming part.

I walked into the Black Bull Tavern and took a seat the bar. The same bartender from last night was working again and he turned to me with a smile.

"Ah, where's yer young lass?" he asked.

"I don't have a lass."

"Then the young lady on yer arm last night."

"We work together."

"Ah, complicated. I understand." I brushed him off and took a menu.

CHAPTER 23

Lisey

I ran to my room and launched myself through the door as I ran out the room without so much as putting my panties on. My chest heaving

as I closed the door quickly behind me and threw the lights on. I went into the bathroom and turned the water on, getting it as hot as I was able. Curling up on the floor of the shower, I let the tears of embarrassment flow into the water.

The rest of the day had went by in a total blur. I didn't remember how I got from one place to the next. It was like I was on autopilot and my body was going through the motions.

It was after we wrapped up for the day, that I decided to call Aggie and tell her what happened. As I waited for her to answer, the tears fell again, mirrored in the screen.

She answered.

"What the fuck happened?" Aggie asked.

"Aggie, it's been awful," I sobbed.

"Tell me what's going on."

"I don't know. We were doing stuff and getting to that point and then when he started to stick his dick in, I freaked out."

"Why?"

"I don't know." I shoved my face into my pillow as tears of embarrassment flooded my eyes.

"You almost had Quinn Rose as your first fuck."

"I know, but we are working together. He's basically my boss."

"Is that what freaked you out?"

"I don't know," I groaned as I pulled my head from the pillow and stared at her through the screen. "I screwed everything up."

"What happened? After you said stop?"

"He stopped. He threw himself off the bed as though I had launched him from a cannon. I didn't give him any time to say anything, and I didn't stick around to explain."

"Lis, it's okay. It was your first time."

"But I feel so stupid." I felt my voice crack as I tried to hold back the abundance of tears.

"You aren't stupid. You were scared, that's normal."

"Why do I feel this way?"

"Because you're embarrassed." I rolled over on to my side, resting my head against the pillow as I looked at her through the screen.

"This is going to make things awkward."

"Don't let it. You are still sexy as fuck; you keep your head up and remind him that he isn't shit to you." I nodded, she had a point, but I felt a twist in my stomach that could make me vomit. "You are Ellisia Hammond; no man will make you feel inferior." I nodded. "Say it."

"I'm Ellisia Hammond and no man will make me feel inferior."

"Louder."

"I am Ellisia Hammond, and no man will make me feel inferior," I said loudly.

"That's my girl," Aggie said with a smile. There came a knocking on the wall from Quinn's room. I shuddered slightly.

"Shit."

"Fuck him. He isn't shit." I nodded. "What are you doing tonight?"

"Nothing as of now, was going to call you and then probably go to sleep early, they are scheduled for another reading in the morning and then we are supposed to go check out the sets."

"You should get a drink after the day you had; you earned it."

"I really shou." I stopped as a knock came at my door.

"Who is it?" Aggie asked.

"I don't know, I'm still sitting here with you," I whispered.

"Well go answer it."

"What if it's him?"

"So, what if it is? You don't owe him anything with the way he treated you today, maybe if he had been nicer then you could have explained. You don't owe him a single fucking thing." I nodded.

"I'll call you back." She nodded and ended the chat. I got up and padded over to the door. As I pulled it open, Quinn was standing there with a bellhop at his side. I pushed my glasses up as they had slid down my nose. He was shirtless, his muscles tight as his chest heaved.

"What can I do for you, Mr. Rose?" He slapped the shoulder of the bellhop beside him.

"This is Derbin, he's going to help you move your stuff."

"Move my stuff?" I asked puzzled.

"They are moving your room. You're loud and disrupting me."

"I've done noth."

"Thanks Derbin, for helping Miss Hammond, relocate to her new room, on the third floor," he interrupted.

"The third flo."

"Have a good night Miss Hammond," he interrupted again. He cocked me a crooked smile and walked away leaving me in defeat. His door slammed and I looked at Derbin.

"I have your new room key miss, where are your bags?" I stood back and welcomed him inside. Quickly, I ran around the room and tossed everything into the bag, zipping it part way. I grabbed my phone and tucked it in the back pocket of my shorts, before grabbing my gown and toiletries together, a clutter in my arms. Derbin met me at the door.

The elevator ride felt like it was descending into hell. I was fuming over the situation. I was neither loud nor disruptive; this was an act of retaliation.

As the elevator doors opened, my cheeks went red, when I saw several well-dressed couples waiting on the elevator. I was standing there in pajama shorts, a tank top, and my fuzzy slippers. I hurried past them as Derbin led me down the hallway, with my head down. I could hear them snickering behind me. My cheeks flashed with embarrassment.

Derbin opened the door to my new room and led me inside. It wasn't nearly as nice as the other room. It had a small window that looked over the back alleyway. He put my bag down and nodded at me.

"Thank you, Derbin. I'm sorry for the interruption."

"It's quite alright Miss, have a good night." I nodded and he left the room. The sound of the door clicking shut behind him felt so final. I looked around the room and the question of whether I was going to survive this job came to mind. It wasn't the room that was the problem, it was my newly appointed boss.

I hung my dress up in the small armoire and set my toiletries up in the bathroom. I sat on the bed, and it squeaked loudly. I felt tears coming to my eyes as I rang Aggie back.

"What happened?" she asked as she popped onto my screen.

"He had me moved."

"What the fuck do you mean he had you moved?"

"He complained to the front desk that I was loud and disruptive and demanded that they move me."

"What a fucking little bitch." I opened my mouth to breathe but could no longer hold back the tears that I was so desperately trying to hide. "Don't cry, Lis."

"How am I supposed to do this? My one big chance and I'm screwing it up already."

"You didn't screw anything up."

"I don't think I can work with him like this. He clearly hates me."

"Then hate him back."

"How do I do that?"

"You do as he ask, but you give him a dose of his own medicine. Don't let him see you break and eventually, he will realize that what he says and does no longer affects you and he'll stop."

"Do you think that will work?"

"I'm counting on it." I took a deep shaky breath. Aggie sighed. "You got this Lis. You have been working your ass off for so long to get here. No, it's not what you were promised, but you are still there. Just think about it, you get to work with Ludwig."

"You're right."

"Get some sleep, lovie, I'll talk to you tomorrow." I nodded.

"Love you, Agg."

"Love you too, Lis."

"Goodnight."

"Goodnight." She ended the call, and I fell back against my pillows. Tears silently falling down the sides of my face. I took my glasses off and rubbed my eyes, before placing them on the nightstand.

As I rolled over and burrowed into the stiff sheets. My train of thought was derailed instantly when I heard a bumping on the wall behind my headrest. I lifted my head and listened closely. A moan came from behind the wall, and I groaned as I flopped my head back down on the pillow and covered it. The moaning and banging got louder. It was going to be a long fucking night.

CHAPTER 24

Quinn

I had several beers and shots before I even had dinner in front of me.

"That kind of complicated aye?" Owen asked. I ignored him and threw back another shot. He placed my dinner in front of me, and I felt my stomach begin to grumble. I forgot to have Lisey order my lunch today and so I didn't eat. I drank it instead at the hotel bar.

To avoid more questions from Owen, I ate quickly and then headed out the door, back to the hotel.

After my shower, I sprawled out on my bed, butt ass naked. My chest heaving as I thought about all the things that had happened the night before.

My thoughts were broken when my phone began to ring. My heart leapt out of my chest, and I scrambled to reach it. Sighing heavily when I saw Barry's name come across the screen.

"What's up, Barry?"

"How's Edinburgh?" My mind flashed to my face buried between Lisey's thighs, her squirming as sweet sounds came from her mouth. I instantly felt my dick grow hard.

"It's alright."

"How's the movie?"

"We haven't even gone to set yet."

"What happened with that girl you met on the plane; did you go out with her?"

"You could say that." I grumbled.

"What do you mean?"

"She's my assistant."

"No way!"

"Don't get excited, Barry."

"When did you find out?"

"That night, before we were set to meet for our date."

"Are you going to bang her?" My mind drifted back to the night before, the way she bit her lip as I stared down at her flashed through my mind.

"That wouldn't be professional."

"Since when are you professional? You dick down anything that gets you harder than a rock."

"Well, this is different Barry. This isn't another show at any venue. We will be working together for the next several months."

"You should still get that ass though."

"I have other things to worry about."

"Have you met Marina yet?"

"Yes, I sat next to her at dinner, and we will be sitting next to each other at the readings from now until set. Then we will be shooting most days together."

"That's so sick. You need to see if you can get with her people about setting up a tour."

"I thought Roddy, was working on that? She brought it up to me last night at dinner."

"He is, but they never respond." I smiled slightly.

"I'll see if I can't work my magic." It was then that I heard something coming through the wall. I pulled the phone away from my ear and heard a voice coming through the wall. Her voice. I put the phone to my ear again.

"Hang on a second, Barry." I raised my fist and knocked hard against the wall. "I'll have to call you back, bro."

"Don't worry about it, call me tomorrow."

"Copy that." The call ended and I grabbed my room phone.

"Front desk."

"Hi, this is Quinn Rose in six-thirty-three, I need you to relocate my neighbor, they are being loud and disruptive, and I have an early day tomorrow." I held the phone between my shoulder and my ear as I pulled on a pair of basketball shorts.

"Which neighbor?"

"Six-thirty-five."

"Right away, Mr. Rose. We will send someone up there to help relocate them immediately."

"Thank you."

It wasn't much longer that I heard a knock in the hallway coming from outside the next door.

I walked out and saw a bellhop waiting. I joined him.

"Thank you for doing this." I read his nametag. "Derbin." He nodded.

The door opened and Lisey was standing there, her curly hair a mess, her glasses hanging on the end of her nose, wearing a tank top and a pair of shorts. I could see her nipples were hard behind her tank top and I had to throw out all reason to keep my member from growing.

"What can I do for you, Mr. Rose?" It came out innocently. I slapped my hand against Derbin's shoulder as he stood beside me.

"This is Derbin, he's going to help you move your stuff."

"Move my stuff?" She seemed puzzled.

"They are moving your room. You're loud and disrupting me."

"I've done noth."

"Thanks Derbin, for helping Miss Hammond, relocate to her new room, on the third floor," I interrupted, giving her no room to ask questions. I had to get away from her, my eyes kept glancing down to her chest and I could feel my dick aching to come free from my shorts.

"The third flo."

"Have a goodnight, Miss Hammond." I walked away and went back to my room, the door clicking shut behind me. I felt a smile creep into the corners of my mouth.

Taking my shorts off, I got into bed, rolling onto my back and taking my aching member into my hand and stroking it. My head pushed back into the pillows as I relived every moment she was in my bed the night before.

After the agonizing release, I stood up and walked to the mirror, panting as I leaned on the sink. I stared deep into my own eyes.

"This can never happen again. She said stop, which means we move on." As the words came out of my mouth there was an ache in my stomach. I shoved the feeling away and turned to lean against the sink and stare into the darkness of the room. The faint light of the city beyond the window, lacing a dim glow in the night. I crossed my arms over my chest. It was for the best, for Lisey and for me. I had been through this a few times with other women, but the panic she exuded was something that I had never seen before. I had never had a woman panic and run like she had, usually they said no, we stopped and then they gathered their things in silence and left quietly.

My heart began to ached with the thought. What could have happened to her that made her react that way? No one just freaks out like that and runs without any explanation. Then again, it's not like a gave her time to explain anything at all.

The way she held herself in the bed, flashed before my eyes and I turned back towards the mirror. I had worked too hard to get where I was, I wasn't going to lose it all because of this girl. She was beautiful, clothed, unclothed, it didn't matter, but she didn't want me, and I wasn't going to let myself slide backwards because of her. She was just another girl in a lengthy list. Sure, I didn't get to conquer her the way I wanted, but this conquest was now over.

***

When I woke up in the morning, it was to the sound of my phone instead of the knocking on the door, from my assistant. I sat up and rolled over, irritated that the time on the phone was just a little after four in the morning. Groaning, I pulled myself from the bed and headed for the shower.

The scalding water cascaded down my body as I tried not to fall back asleep. My head resting against the wall. Water dripping down the front of my face as I stood their staring.

I could have stayed there forever if it weren't for the knocking I heard at the door. I grumbled and stepped out. I didn't bother grabbing a towel, instead I headed straight for the handle.

As I pulled it open, I felt a smile creep into the corner of my lips.

"Good morning, Mr. Oh God." She averted her eyes and turned away quickly. I leaned in the door frame.

"Good morning, Miss Hammond. What can I do for you?"

"They are preparing to head to set early today. They want to read on site. The cars will be loading soon, and they plan to leave in fifteen minutes." She kept her hand up, blocking her eyes as her head was turned down the hallway and I was merely amused.

"Is that all?" I asked slowly.

"Yes."

"Thank you, Miss Hammond." It came out slower than I intended and I watched her cheeks go red, before she darted off down the hallway and around the corner.

CHAPTER 25

Lisey

I bolted down the hallway to the elevator as fast as my legs would carry me. I had gotten a glimpse of what Quinn was packing. My cheeks went red at the thought, as my mind raced back to that night, where I looked like a complete fool. My head dropped.

I didn't pick it up again until I reached the bottom floor.

"Miss Hammond," Jafe said as he approached me.

"He's on his way down, he won't be long."

"That's fine and dandy, but I need you to do something else today. Far more important."

"What's that?"

"Today you will work with Ludwig on set. He doesn't like the way the team has things set up and he needs help working on the dialogue. He said since you are here and came highly recommended, he wanted to work with you personally and see what you got." My heart practically stopped in my chest.

"He requested me?"

"Yes. Is that alright, Miss Hammond?" I nodded my head quickly, excitement building in my chest. This was my chance.

"Where is he right now?"

"He is currently on set. I can have a car take you to him." I nodded and he led me towards the front doors.

Down the steps, there was car waiting and he opened the door for me. He leaned his head in.

"Can you please take Miss Hammond to set to join Mr. Ludwig?" The driver nodded and he Jafe turned to me. "We will see you in a little bit, Miss Hammond."

"Thank you, Jafe." He closed the door, and the car took off into the busy streets of Edinburgh.

When we arrived on site, we were outside of the city, rolling atop green hills extended as far as the eye could see. The small village of Juniper Green, down below. I got out of the car and walked over to a tented area, where a bench had been set up. At the bench I found Mr. Ludwig, sitting with his leg crossed over the other with the script in hand. He turned to me, his silvery moustache and beard, a gleam hidden behind his glass framed eyes.

"You must be Miss Hammond." The way he said my name sent a shiver down my spine. This man was literally everything legendary in my world and he was sitting right in front of me.

"Yes, sir."

"Please, call me Lou." He gestured to the open spot on the bench next to him and I quickly took a seat. I could feel my heart pounding as I watched him stare off into the hills, waiting impatiently for him to say something.

It was then he leaned over to me, the script open in his hand, showing me where to look.

"What is this scene missing?" he asked. I looked over the script. The scene was set to be the one where Ayaan treks over the hills of the highlands, fresh from prison, gearing up to get back to Edinburgh to settle the score. Looking at it, it seemed very bland, like it was missing something. It just said he walks over the hills.

"We need to move the tent," I said.

"Tell me more."

"If we move the tent and wait until just the right moment, we can get the shot of him coming over the hill as the sun breaks the crest, looking down at the village as it's still covered in darkness. I would also monologue, give context to his life before this moment." I was staring off and the silence brought me back down. I looked at him and he was beaming.

"I knew you would be a good choice for this Miss Hammond." I smiled and he looked out to where I had been staring.

"Boys!" he bellowed. Three men came flying from inside the tent. "Get this tent moved." They began to say something, their accents so thick it was hard for me to decipher, but they began to move things out from inside the tent and get it torn down.

"Won't Director Hardy be upset?" I asked.

"Old Mage? No. I will tell him exactly why. This isn't our first movie together. We have worked together long enough for him to know better than to question my changes." A nagging question began to burn inside of me. I was sitting here with a legend, who had quietly stolen my position.

"Can I ask why you waited so long to join the production?'"

"I was working on another set. The internet is terrible in Prague, so I was a little behind on my communications." I smiled at his answer but that smile soon faded.

"I asked them to keep you here." I looked at him. "Lou?"

"They wanted to send you home when they heard that I was coming and I told them that I would need an assistant, and you obviously are highly recommended if you are who they chose when I didn't respond." I tipped my feet up and pushed my heels back down again.

"Thank you," I said quietly. He patted my hands as they sat in my lap.

"Thank you for staying. I can tell already that you are going to be a wonderful addition to the team." I couldn't help but smile again as my cheeks grew red.

We sat there and continued going through the script, working on the monologue as the crew behind us dismantled the tent.

"So is screenwriting a career you want to pursue?" Lou asked.

"Actually, I'd like to publish my own novel someday."

"So why not start?"

"I have; I just haven't finished."

"You should finish it."

"I plan too, but it's hard with working right now."

"You'll miss every shot if you don't live."

"What do you mean?"

"If you work to live, but don't live, you aren't really living at all."

"I'm confused."

"You'll understand one day when you're older," he smiled.

"I'm twenty-four."

"Like I said, older."

When the production crew and the cast arrived, the sun was barely fully pass the horizon. I watched as the cars pulled up and felt a twist in my gut at the sight of Quinn. His eyes quickly finding mine, with an intense glare, before striding up to me with the surge of an angry bear.

"Where the hell did you go? I've been calling you." I stood pulling my phone out of my back pocket and saw that there were several missed calls.

"I'm sorry, Mr. Rose, I mu."

"Sorry nothing. You are my assistant are you not?" He interrupted. I felt my shoulders shake under his words. To think that a few days ago he seemed so sweet and kind up until he didn't get his way and this was who he really was. His true colors bright not just in front of me but in front of Lou as well. I kept my face hard as stone, squaring my shoulders as I felt my insides crumble, a cold chill wisping through my body until I felt the warm hands of Lou as he placed them on my shoulders. I turned to look at him.

"I asked them to bring her because I needed her help. I'm George Ludwig, the lead screenwriter." He removed a hand from my shoulder and extended it to him. Quinn took it and cocked a smile as he looked at me.

"So, you're the one who took Miss Hammond's job?" He cackled, and I felt my lungs deflate immediately. The hurt had to have been easily written across my face at this point. I could feel the tears welling in the back of my eyes and I pushed them away. I had worked hard for this, to be here, to now learn from him. I wasn't going to let this petty fuckboy ruin my chances.

"Mr. Rose, is there something you need presently?" I asked with a plastered smile on my face. His grin weakened until there was nothing left. "Lou and I have a lot of work to do to get this scene prepared to shoot before we lose the light. If you'll excuse us." Lou locked his arm with mine and nodded at Quinn as we walked away. Leaving him there dumbfounded. Lou leaned over to me.

"That was smashing. You really gave it right back to him. Are you alright?" He wasn't oblivious to the tears that I had forced back, as they now trickled slightly down my face, leaving warmth tracing down my skin in jagged patterns.

"I'm sorry. I just snapped."

"Not to worry. I was going to say something if you didn't." I smiled slightly.

Once the tent was finally moved, we entered inside to join the others for a quick reading.

"My goal is to get the opening shot done today. Mr. Ludwig, what are your ideas for this scene?"

Lou looked at me and put his hand on my shoulder.

"Miss Hammond, has envisioned the opening scene and if we want to get the right lighting, we need to get on set quickly." My eyes scanned the faces that sat around the table, catching Quinn's as he rolled them at the sound of my name.

"Miss Hammond, has point, alright people let's move." Everyone rose from their seats as Director Hardy approached us. As I scanned my eyes to meet his face, I saw Quinn staring at me not quick to get up at all. I jumped slightly as Director Hardy took my hand.

"Tell me your vision."

"As the sun rises over the highlands, Ayaan, walks over the crests and stares down at the village just below, his old home, long have they forgotten him, now back to settle the score. We added a monologue to captivate the moment." He grinned from ear to ear.

"I love it. Mr. Rose." We turned and looked at Quinn as he remained seated, he shifted his gaze lazily to us.

"Yes, Director Hardy?"

"Get to your dressing room, we need you screen ready in ten minutes." I watched as Quinn rose slowly from his seat, pushing back the sleeves of his white button-down shirt as his eyes glazed over me. As they flicked up to meet mine, he shot a cocky side smile, before heading out the door. A chill raced through my body and suddenly, I felt the faintness of his touch from the other night.

"Lisey?" I looked at Lou. "Are you alright?"

"Yeah, I'm fine."

"Let's get the scene set." I nodded and followed him outside.

CHAPTER 26

Quinn

I walked into my trailer and was practically ambushed by a team of costume designers and makeup artists.

"We have to move quickly; Hardy wants you on set as soon as possible." I nodded irritated and took a seat.

As I sat there and let them mess with my hair and prep my face, my mind floundered back to the encounter with Lisey when I arrived. The way she straightened herself and spoke back to me. It was probably the hottest thing she had done so far, and it took everything in me, to control the ache in my groin. My eyes snapped up to the mirror.

"Knock it off Quinn. She's no longer on the radar; you need to find a new plaything." My brain was berating me behind my eyes, and I could feel it.

Shortly, they were pulling me up out of the chair and I was having clothes put into my hands. I looked down at them, and it was pretty standard, hoodie, jeans, and work boots.

Changing quickly, I found myself looking in the mirror again. I had to forget about her. This was the move of my career; I couldn't let her get under my skin or under me. I had to get rid of her, because having her here was going to ruin my chances at stardom. She was a distraction that I couldn't afford. There was a light rap at the door that pulled me away as I had my shirt halfway unbuttoned. I walked to the trailer door and pulled it open.

"Mr. Rose." There she stood, in the dim embrace of the growing dawn. Daylight was approaching.

"What?" I asked sharply. She flinched slightly and I felt a pull inside my heart, something that faintly felt like regret. I had to push it down. I couldn't let her distract me. I was going to have to find a reason to fire her.

"We are ready for you on set and if we want to get the right shot we have to hurry." Her eyes were locked with mine and I leaned in the doorway, watching them trace down to my open chest.

"Eyes up here, Miss Hammond," I sighed. Her eyes snapped back to meet mine and I saw a flush of red in her cheeks. "I'll be out in a few moments." She nodded and I shut the door, shrouding her in darkness.

"That was a dick move," I said out loud. But necessary. I had to get her off this project and out of my head.

When I arrived on set, I was hurriedly moved around to get into position. The cameras were set up, other accenting lights were in place, and everyone was scurrying to get out of the frame. I looked around as I walked and saw Lisey with Hardy and Ludwig, near the camera. She was checking her phone. Probably trying to determine how much time we had. Hardy snapped his eyes up to mine and then strode over. He fell into step with me as we walked towards the crest of the hill.

"In this scene I need you to really give me what you got. You were just freed from prison and walked all the way back home. You're tired, hungry, and ready to get back into the ring. I want to see that fire in your eyes, but the evidence of exhaustion on your face.

As we crested the hill, I could see the sun beginning on the horizon. There wouldn't be much time to get this shot, there wouldn't be room for mistakes.

"I'll be on the other side. The crew will let you know when to start walking."

"Yes, sir." I shot him a sideways smile.

"I would like to get this in one shot if we can."

"I understand." He clapped my shoulder.

"Good lad." He turned away and went back over the hill. I watched him as he disappeared. I turned my attention back to the glow that was coming off the distance. Reminding myself of who I was in the moment. I wasn't Quinn right now. I was Ayaan Lawson, wrongfully imprisoned for a murder that I didn't commit. I knew I was innocent and now I had to return to where it all happened and prove it, while fighting to get the life that was taken from me back.

"Action!" I began to briskly walk up to the crest of the hill, getting my chest pumping so that my breath was batted when I reached the top.

As I gazed over at the village below, I was met with tons of cameras and cascaded lights combating to aid the shot. I looked down at the village and sighed heavily, letting the fog emanate from between my lips as my shoulders dropped with relief.

"Cut!" A siren wailed and I looked down towards Hardy. He stood from his chair and motioned for me to join him. As I walked over I caught a glimpse of Lisey whispering quietly with Ludwig.

"Good work kid," Hardy said as I approached, he point the camera, and he replayed it. The scene came in with me walking over the hill and the camera zoomed in on my face, the sun had risen behind me, and the emotions on my face were palpable.

"I love it!" Hardy yelled. "That's a wrap on the opening scene everyone! We are in business!" There were cheers coming from all around and my eyes trailed to Lisey, she glanced at me briefly before turning back to the conversation she was having. I felt my member twitch in my pants as her green eyes had drifted to me and then away quickly. I studied her face for a moment seeing if there was anything else. My mind reeling trying to calm down what was happening in my pants. She had to go.

Marina and Branigan showed up awhile later to do readings. The tents and cameras had been packed up and moved closer to the village as our next few shots would be shot on scene within the cobblestone walls. It was a small village no more than a couple hundred people living there. There was a coffee shop, a small grocery store and a library, the rest of the village had houses and various shops with one pub.

I was relieved when we returned to the hotel, it was a little after eight o'clock. It had been a long day, and I needed a shower. I stepped out of the car that had driven me too and from set. As I ascended the steps towards the door of the hotel, the car pulled away, and another pulled up. I turned to look at the black BMW that had pulled up. I waited to see who would get out when I saw a well-dressed man remove himself from the driver's seat, he walked around the front of the car and approached the passenger side, opening the door.

"Mr Rose." I turned and Lisey was standing in front of me, her brown curls pinned up in a delicate bundle on her head, a black cocktail dress that stopped just at the knees adorned her delectable body. I eyed her up and down briefly.

"Miss Hammond." It almost came out as a question.

"Excuse me," she said as her eyes locked with mine. I stepped aside in a daze and watched her descend the stairs. The gentleman at the curb, held firmly to the door as they greeted each other, leaning in to plant a kiss on her cheek. I felt a rush of rage surging in my chest, filling my face with a burning desire to rip her back and slam my lips against her. She slid into the car, and he closed the door. Eying me he nodded and then returned around the side to the driver side, getting in, they sped off down the road.

The heat in my face led to a low growl in my throat. Part of me wanted to hail a cab and follow them. Suddenly, I felt a shift in the world around me. She was never mine to have. She had someone else already, despite my desire for her, as the questions of our night together resurfaced, I huffed and stalked off into the hotel.

I slammed down on my bed, the wetness of my body soaking into the sheets as I pushed the phone to my ear as it rang.

"Hey bro," Barry said.

"I have to get rid of this girl."

"What's going on?"

"She just waltzed out of here with another guy."

"And that bothers you why?" His question struck me hard, like being hit with a baseball bat.

"I have no idea. I need to get her off this project so I can focus."

"Fire her."

"I need a reason, she's also working with Ludwig, and she ran point on the scene today which Hardy loved. He's not going to let me get rid of her so easily."

"Make something up."

"Like what?"

"Say she stole something."

"She's definitely not the type."

"Well, it's either her or you." He was right, if I didn't get her off this project or at least quell my desires for her, she was going to ruin this for me, and I was going to lose my chance.

"I'm definitely not quitting."

"Then she's got to go."

CHAPTER 27

Lisey

"Who was that guy?" Archie asked as we drove down the road. My mind was a flurry with my brush with Quinn.

"That's my boss."

"That arsehole you told me about?"

"The very same."

"Want me to deck him for ye?"

"No. That would definitely have me packing and going back home or at least hiding out at dad's until my boss was ready to welcome me back. Failure isn't an option for me, Arch." He nodded.

"Fear not, cousin. Should he give ye any trouble ye let me ken."

"I will." He pulled up outside of a fancy restaurant. A valet waited at the curb, and he stopped the car. The valet opened my door and offered me a hand.

"Good evening, ma'am." I nodded at him as I took his hand, and he helped me from the car. Archie came around the front of the car and handed him the keys before pushing a note into his hand.

"Thank you."

"You're welcome, sir." The valet disappeared to move the car and Archie walked up to the door, opening it, holding his hand out for me to enter.

"Cousin," he said. I nodded my head and entered the restaurant.

As we sat at the table, champagne was poured in crystal flutes that adorned the table, a beautiful flower arrangement sat low on the table, candles lit in the center. I poured over the menu, but I was distracted by Quinn's eyes as they traced up and down my body. The memory sending chills rushing over my skin, making my stomach turn. The haunting memories of the night we spent together resurfaced and I felt my cheeks go red.

"What is it?" My thoughts broke as Archie spoke to me.

"Nothing," I said pushing the thoughts away and forcing my mind to focus on the menu in my hand.

"Anything looking good?"

"The duck sounds nice," I said quietly. I heard him shift and I looked up as he put his menu down. He motioned for the waiter, and one quickly appeared almost out of thin air.

"Can we get a bottle of the Macallan sherry and two orders of the duck please." The writer scribbled away on a black leather-bound notebook in his hand.

"Right away, sir." He reached for the menu in front of Archie, and I gently handed him mine. He disappeared like a wisp, a gentle breeze trailing in his wake.

"Isn't that really expensive?" I asked.

"So, what if it is?" Archie asked as he reached for his flute of champagne.

"You don't have to impress me cousin; this dinner is far too much already." He scoffed and tilted his head, raising his glass.

"Nothing is too fancy for my American cousin, it has been far too long, and this dinner is to celebrate you accomplishment on this project you are working." He gave me a wink, and I picked up my glass, the crystal lips clinking against each other with a pitched ting.

As we finished dinner, the bill arrived, Archie quickly threw some folded notes into the pocket-book and then stood.

"Shall we?" I nodded, my belly was full, and the whiskey was making my head swim. I stood slowly from my chair, making sure that I had my bearings.

As we exited the restaurant the valet approached with the keys in hand, the car running soundlessly at the curb.

"Have a good night sir, ma'am," he said as he bowed his head to us.

"You too." Archie said. We approached the car, and Archie opened the passenger side door for me. I nodded my head in thanks as I slid in. He closed the door, pulling the buckle across my lap, snapping it into place.

As we pulled up in front of the hotel, my heart quickened when I saw Quinn just outside the hotel door. He was leaning against the wall, a look on his face that I recognized as intoxication illuminating in the light. He was blocked as Archie appeared in the window as he opened my door. I gently took his offered hand and stood on the sidewalk. He leaned towards me, and I pushed out my cheek, before turning to kiss his as well.

"Goodnight, Lis."

"Night, Arch. Thank you for tonight. I had a wonderful time."

"When you have a few days off, we will have to go to my parents in the country. I know they are looking forward to seeing you." My eyes met his and I nodded.

"I would love to see them too; I'll send you my schedule." He nodded and then disappeared around the car again as I headed up the stairs. I was ready to confront Quinn; I wanted to know what the hell had happened earlier as I was leaving.

I ascended the steps with great purpose and determination, forming the words exactly in my head as each step sent a reverberation through my body.

Merely steps away from opening my mouth to expel them and I stopped dead as a beautiful red head appeared, leaning against him. His head tipped down, his mouth locking with hers, his hands tracing down her back to her ass, squeezing it. I could hear the heat of their shared kiss as she moaned loudly, and my cheeks instantly went red. I put my head down and squeaked by them quickly, hoping that he was far too distracted by his new friend to notice me. I grabbed the handle of the door.

"Miss Hammond," he slurred. I stopped, and against my better judgement I turned to look at him. The woman was draped around his neck, looking at me as his messy hair curled in front of his face just barely above his eyes.

"Do not disturb me tomorrow." He turned his attention to the girl leaning against him and traced his thumb along her chin. "I'll be sleeping in." He laughed as he peered down at her. I felt a tinge of pain rise in my stomach. I nodded my head, keeping it held high, his eyes turning back meeting mine. My eyes exuded defiance. I wasn't going to let him get to me, he could be the largest asshole in the world and the biggest dick, but I was determined to come out on top of this. I just had to get through this shoot and then I would never have to see him again.

"Is that all, Mr. Rose?" He shook his head, before turning his attention back to the woman.

"Bring two coffees, say around ten."

"Director Hardy wants everyone on set by eight," I protested.

"Crew not cast. I expect the coffee at ten."

"But I won't be here."

"Are you trying to dismiss your duties as my assistant?" he asked, his voice laced with venom.

"No, but I am expected with Ludwig tomorrow."

"Coffee. Ten."

"Will you fire me if not?"

"I could," he laughed. I felt a pit forming in my stomach. I couldn't lose this job. I sighed in annoyance rather than defeat.

"I'll do my best, Mr. Rose." He waved me off and I entered the hotel. A smile creased in the corner of my lips. Alright Quinn, you want to play a game than I'm all for it. With the plan already formed in my mind I walked up to the counter and began discussing with the clerk.

"Can I have two coffees delivered to room three-thirty-three, at ten in the morning please?"

"How would you like those, ma'am? Sugar? Cream? Honey?" I smiled as the word slithered from my lips. He liked his coffee, like his aura.

"Black."

CHAPTER 28

Quinn

I was awoken by a knocking on the door. I rolled over and was met by the naked red head. She had fallen asleep on my arm, after our multiple rounds of romping. I pulled it from underneath her and wrapped a towel around my waist before answering the door.

"Miss Hammond, you're late," I said as I pulled the door open with quelled agitation. To my surprise it wasn't Lisey at the door, but instead a hotel employee with a tray in hand.

"You're morning coffee, sir." He held the tray up to me and I took the two coffees.

"Where is the young woman who usually brings me my coffee?" I asked. I didn't know if he would know who I was talking about, but I sent her down every morning, and even throughout the day just to keep her out of my hair.

"She went with the rest of the crew early this morning. A car has been arranged to take you to set and another one arranged for your guest," he said as he nodded into the room. I turned as the red head who's name I couldn't remember stirred, rustling the sheets.

"When will the cars arrive?"

"Withing several minutes, sir." I nodded in thanks and shut the door. I walked over and handed her the coffee.

"See you tonight?" she asked.

"No. I have a prior engagement. I'll call you." She nodded and reached out touching my face before kissing me gently on the lips. I knew I wasn't going to call her, I never even gave her my number, but I knew she had been so drunk the previous night she wouldn't bother checking to see if she had it.

***

As I arrived on set the crew was setting up around the village, placing everything where they wanted it to be. I glanced across the heavy work that was being done and saw Lisey giving instructions to one of the setup guys. I stalked over to her.

Her curly brown hair was piled on top of her head in a messy bun; stray strands framed her face. If it weren't for the amount of people around I would have probably grabbed her by the hair.

"You didn't bring me coffee this morning." My words dripping with anger. To be honest, I didn't care, but this was the exact thing I needed to get rid of her.

"Did you not get it this morning?" she asked defiantly.

"It came to my room, but it wasn't from you."

"I told you I wasn't going to be there."

"But I told you to bring it to me."

"I made arrangements to have it brought to you, and it was, therefore, you got your coffee," she said smugly as she rolled her eyes. She locked her hips as she crossed her arms over her chest.

"You're fired." I said. She raised her hand, pressing it to her chest just above her breasts and opened her mouth as though in protest. I nearly felt a sense of satisfaction until she smiled.

"I actually quit this morning."

"Well then, let's get you to the airport." I placed my hand on her lower back and began to swiftly guide her when after two steps she spun out of my reach.

"I didn't quit the production. Just you." She crossed her arms, a smile easing into the corners of her pouty mouth.

"But you're my assistant."

"No, I actually found someone to take that job. Lou wants me working with him for the entire production and Hardy agreed after yesterday's visionary shot." She cocked her head.

"Who is it?" Her piercing eyes glanced passed me and she nodded her chin upwards.

"That should be her now." I turned looking at the car that had just arrived on set. The back door swung open and getting out of the back seat was the same red head I had spent the night with. I spun on Lisey, fuming.

"What did you do?"

"I figured since you both are getting on so well that you two would work splendidly together. Her voice was taunting; it was taking everything in my not to bend her over my knee.

"Hi, Quinn!" A high-pitched voice called from behind me. I turned my head and gave a slight wave, before turning back to Lisey, shooting daggers at her.

"Her names Ayda, in case you forgot." A low growl emanated from my chest. She perked up with a large smile. Her voice mocking Ayda's pleasantly pitched tone. "See you on set, Q." With that she turned away, sauntering down the street. Fuming, I watched as she joined Ludwig, and they entered the coffee shop. I felt a presence behind me and took a deep breath before turning around. The Scottish girl from last night stood a few feet away from me beaming.

"Hello again, Ayda."

"Thank you so much," she said instantly.

"For what?"

"For getting me this job. I saw the note and the flowers when I got into the car. I thought they were going to take me home, but they said they were bringing me here. I'm actually quite surprised by your kind gesture." I rubbed my forehead with my thumb and forefinger, a headache beginning. Not only did she get this girl hired to be my assistant, but she also turned it around to make it seem like it was my idea.

The clever minx. I could wrap my hands around her neck if she were still standing here. The thought aroused me, sending a heat coiling through my groin, and itch that I was determined to leave unscratched. The situation was far from my style, but I would have to make do. If it was war she wanted, then it was war she was going to get.

CHAPTER 29

Lisey

"**Y**ou. Did. Not!" Aggie squealed through the screen of my tablet. I was sitting cross legged on my bed in my pajamas as the quiet sounds of the city filtered in through the window.

"I did."

"You bad bitch, you finally came to play hardball. I'm so fucking proud of you!"

"You should have seen the look on his face after he saw her standing there."

"I bet it was priceless."

"I wish I would have had my camera; it would have been the perfect souvenir."

"I would have paid big money to see his face."

"Aggie, it was truly a perfect moment. He thought he was just going to fire me, like I wasn't already three steps ahead of him."

"The smug bastard." I felt my smile fade as the room fell silent between us.

"Are you okay?" she asked. My mind kept going back to that night, the way his hands touched me all over, the way he worked his tongue between my thighs. I felt a touch of guilt for what I had done.

"Don't you dare." Aggie's voice broke me from my thoughts.

"What?"

"I know that face," she said accusingly.

"What face?"

"The face of regret. You don't owe him a damn thing. You guys had a little fun; you stopped it and he's been treating you like fucking shit ever since. Nah, fuck him."

"I do feel a little bad though."

"Girl, don't. He's getting everything he deserves." I sucked in a heavy breath, releasing it as I shook out my shoulders.

"You're right."

"You know what you need to do now?"

"What's that?"

"Go find yourself a nice piece of Scottish ass."

"After what happened with Quinn, I think I'm safer not doing that."

"You need to get over it, Lis. You can't change what happened, but you can always change your mind. You need to get laid; you can't stay a virgin forever." I knew she was right, but the truth was I was afraid. I had come so close with Quinn that night and everything felt right, but in the last second I freaked out. I sighed heavily.

"I just need to fucking do it."

"That's right. You just need to fucking do it." I nodded my head and stood on the bed briefly to flip on to my knees, making the tablet bounce.

"I'm going out. I'll call you later."

"Damn right! Love you!"

"Love you too." I ended the call and sashayed to the bathroom to get ready.

As I walked through the hallway, the polished floors squeaked underneath my sneakers. The clerk behind the desk acknowledged me and I nodded in return, before continuing out the door.

I wasn't too familiar with the area, so I settled on going down to the Black Bull. The sidewalk was clear of all human life and there were barely any cars on the street. A sense of urgency wrapped itself around me as I reached an area I noticed was dark as the streetlights had gone out. I stopped, preparing to turn back. Turning suddenly, I slammed into a firm chest, I raised my hands, but large ones wrapped around my wrists. I was shoved back into a dark alleyway, my back slamming against the hard brick exterior of someone's flat.

"Miss Hammond." I didn't recognize the voice, and it was too dark to see their face.

"Who are you?" I asked.

"A fan." I felt my eyes widen in fear as a snicker came from the figure before me.

"I don't know what you're talking about." They leaned in and I could feel their breath on my neck as they inhaled sharply, taking in my scent. I quivered as they pulled away.

"I'm an old friend of your mother, Elenor." A calloused finger trailed down my cheek, sending a shiver down my spine.

"I don't know who that is." They growled lowly.

"Either way." They forcefully grabbed my chin.

"I'll scream." There was a glint from a distant light as I saw the blade near my face.

"Then I'll have to scar up that pretty face of yours." I squeezed my eyes shut as I swallowed hard. I felt the tip of the blade as he pressed it to my skin.

"Hey!" A voice came from across the street. His grip tightened, yet I managed to turn my head. I heard the sound of someone running towards us, and my face was immediately released. I watched as the mysterious man disappeared down the alleyway into the darkness. A hand on my arm startled me, making me jump.

"Dinnae fash, lass. It's me, Owen." I didn't realize until I stood still for a moment longer that I was absolutely trembling. He put his arm around me.

"Let's get ye to the pub, I'll call for your cousin."
I took two steps as my body quivered. My legs
gave way beneath me and Owen caught me, hoist-
ing me up in his arms as he continued walking. I
leaned my head into his chest, his heavy footfalls
kept pace despite my added weight. Tears lingered
in my eyes as the realization of what had just transpired played back in my head.

Inside the bar, I felt the stares of the regular
crowd as he sat me down on one of the bar stools.

"Here ye are lass, safe." I nodded and folded
my arms on the counter as I leaned against the
bar. My shoulders still shaking. Owen disappeared
through a set of doors and then was immediately
in front of me, pouring me a shot of whiskey. He
slid the glass in front of me, and I gently reached
out and took the glass. He disappeared into the
back.

"Lisey?" I turned my head, and Quinn was sitting at a table in the corner. He was the last person

I needed to see me like this. His chair scraped the floor as he stood, walking briskly towards me.

"What happened?" He asked, a low growl in his voice. I looked up at him, tears were dancing in my eyes, making him look as though he was swimming. I shook my head and looked away from him. Owen reappeared behind the bar; his phone pressed to his ear.

"Arch."

"Lisey's here. Can ye come down?" He looked at me as he eyed Quinn. "Aye." He handed me the phone. "Can ye talk to him?" he asked. I nodded and gently took the phone from him.

"Arch," my voice quivered.

"Lis, are ye alright?"

"Someone attacked me."

"I'm on the way. Ye stay put, ye ken?"

"Okay." With a shaky hand I handed the phone back to Owen. The call had already ended. I could feel a heat on my back as the other patrons stared at me. Owen looked across the bar at them.

"Go on ye bullocks, mind yer own." There were grumbles, but I felt the heat receding. I fumbled for the glass, pulling it to my lips and taking a sip as it quaked in my hand. I felt a warm hand on my shoulder and turned my face, glancing into Quinn's eyes. This man hated me, yet there was sympathy and concern in the way he was looking at me. He picked up his hand and I flinched.

"Hold still," he said gently. He reached for my face, his hand soft as it cupped my chin and his thumb slid along my cheek, hitting a spot that stung, although his touch was gentle. A hiss escaped me, and he pulled his hand away. "You have a cut." I raised my hand and felt the small nick in my cheek, it wasn't deep or exceptionally large, about a quarter of an inch long. I pulled my hand away from my face and observed it as there was a small amount of blood on my index finger. The tears that rimmed my eyes were now falling. I looked back into Quinn's eyes.

"He had a knife," I said shakily. Something flashed in Quinn's eyes, it wasn't just anger, it was pure rage.

CHAPTER 30

Quinn

I was sitting in the corner of the bar, enjoying a nice drink in the quiet. Ayda had been driving me crazy all day and I had been sending her on all sorts of errands to keep her from trying to jump my bones. She wanted to stay the night with me, and I explained to her that now with us working together we couldn't be more than professional with one another. She seemed to understand but continued to ignore it. I needed the cold beer as it slithered down my throat. I placed the glass on the table, just as the front door burst open. Owen walked in with a woman in his arms. He sat her down on a barstool and my heart dropped as I instantly recognized the dark curls.

"Lisey?" She turned her head and at the sight of her face, I was on my feet, walking towards her. Her eyes met mine and they were full of tears.

"What happened?" I wanted to know why she was upset, what had happened to her and who the fuck was going to get their ass kicked. I knew I needed to keep my distance from her, but this was something I never anticipated. My heart fell to pieces as a single tear ran down her face. She shook her head and looked away from me. Owen appeared then.

"Can ye talk to him?" he asked. She nodded and he handed her the phone. My eyes scanned her face as she spoke. Her words lost in the internal fire that was raging in my head.

My eyes landed on a cut on her delicate face.

My blood boiled.

She handed Owen the phone and I reached out.

She flinched slightly.

"Hold still." My voice cracked slightly.

As my thumb traced over the deep red line, she flinched.

Her terrified eyes locked with mine.

"He had a knife." Her voice shattered like glass, dragging my heart through the shards.

My fists clenched, my nails digging deep into my palms as rage filled my chest. I wanted to hit something. Preferably the miserable creature who dared to lay a hand on her.

I couldn't bring myself to say anything.

What could I say?

The door slammed open.

"Lis." I turned and the man who had picked her up the night before rushed towards her. I stepped out of the way, letting him get to her. She wrapped her arms around him as he hugged her tightly, she sobbed into his shoulder.

"Yer alright." He looked up at Owen.

"Thank ye." Owen nodded. I quietly retreated back to my table, where another beer had been placed while I was standing at the bar. I quietly took my seat, pulling the pint close to me as I watched them. He was helping her to her feet.

"Can ye walk?" she nodded, and he put his arm around her shoulders. She tipped her head back, no doubt finishing the whiskey she had in front of her.

"Thank you, Owen." Her voice danced across the quiet space with such a grace that I was almost drawn to get up and go back to her, but I stayed put. The man with her began walking with her towards the door. I watched as it opened and then closed behind them as they disappeared into the night. I got up and walked up to the bar with my drink in hand. I wanted to get back to the hotel and check on her.

"What do I owe you?" I asked.

"We'll settle for ten pounds," Owen replied.

"I had a second pint."

"That yin's was on the pub."

"For what?"

"For being there for the lass." I swallowed hard as her tear-filled eyes flashed in my mind.

"She seemed like she needed someone. Looks like they showed up. I was just here until they got here."

"Arch is a braw lad, and he's pleased she's here." I laid the bill down and slung back the rest of my beer. I set the glass on the counter.

"Thanks, Owen." He nodded and I headed out the door, back to the hotel.

When I got to the third floor, I reached the corner and quickly back pedaled as I saw Lisey standing in the hallway with Arch. He was hugging her.

"Thank you for coming and getting me back safely."

"Anything, Lis. Ye ken?" She nodded. He kissed her cheek and then disappeared down the other end of the hall. She shifted backwards into her room and closed the door behind her. Silence fell in the hallway, and I immediately felt stupid. Going up to that door right now would be a mistake. I turned to walk away, but something tugged at me, and I doubled back. Before I knew it, I was knocking on her door.

I waited for what seemed like forever before the door opened. She was already in her pajamas, her hair pulled back into a high ponytail, her glasses hanging on the bridge of her nose. Our eyes locked and I could see the redness that still remained in her eyes. I reached for her uninjured cheek and a breath hitched in her throat as I cupped it gently.

I lifted ever so slightly, and she tilted her lips up to meet mine. Something sparking between us, she wrapped her arms around my waist, and I let her gently pull me into the room.

She pushed me back against the closed door, locked in a kiss, hot, heavy, exploring one another. I pulled away as she began to tug on my shirt.

"We shouldn't do this." I couldn't believe that those were the words I was saying right now, despite the throbbing of my cock. I wanted her, regardless of what happened between us, regardless of how much I wanted to hate her.

To stay away from her.

There was something greater than myself that was not allowing me to do that, sending something through my body that I hadn't felt in a long time, fear. She continued and I gently took her wrists. Her eyes glimmered in the moonlight of the room as she looked up at me.

"Why?" If it weren't for what had just happened, I would be all over her right now.

"You experienced something traumatic. This would be a mistake." My voice was soft. She backed away from me.

"Why are you here, Quinn?" There was a shake in her voice.

"I came to check on you." She wrapped her arms around herself.

"I'm fine." She was lying, I could tell by the way her voice quivered. I stepped toward her, and she took a step back. "I don't need you to save me." I felt an instant sting on my cheek, like she had reached out and slapped me. She turned away and walked towards the window.

I gently walked up behind her and placed my hands on her shoulders.

"Do you need anything?" She shook her head as she continued looking out at the quiet street below. I squeezed her shoulders gently before letting go, turning to leave.

I was steps away from the door.

"Quinn." I stopped turning. She was still at the window, looking at me now. Tears streaming down her face in the silver moonlight.

"Don't go."

CHAPTER 31

Lisey

When I awoke the next morning, my eyes were sore. I realized by shifting my legs in the bed that Quinn was gone. I could faintly feel his arm still draped over my waist as he stayed with me last night.

"Don't go," I had said. He nodded, and in a few short minutes, we were lying in my bed, his arms around me as I quietly cried myself to sleep.

My mind released the memory as my phone began to ring. I picked it up, and dad was calling. I shot up, panic rising in my chest as I answered the call. I took a quick breath to steady myself.

"Morning, dad." I forced out as cooly as possible.

"Lisey what were you doing out by yourself? Did you see who it was? Are you alright?" Fucking Archie.

"I'm fine, dad." He sighed heavily.

"Open the door, Lis." A shock went through my body, and I looked at the door to my room. I stood up and slowly walked over. Taking the knob, I pulled the door open and there he stood. His hair dappled with silver streaks, his glasses resting high on the bridge of his nose, wearing a nice suit with cufflinks my great grandfather had given him with an intricately designed 'H.' He pulled the phone from his face, and I heard the call end. There wasn't anger or disapproval in his eyes, just the look of a father's tangible fear. His eyes creased at the corners, and my façade broke. Tears streaming down my face as he crossed the threshold and took me in his arms.

"I'm sorry," I sobbed against his chest. He ran a hand through my frizzy curls, as he held me tightly.

"You have nothing to be sorry for."

"He recognized me." Dad pulled away, holding me at arm's length.

"What do you mean?"

"He said he was an old friend of mom's."

"Did you see his face?" I sniffled and shook my head. Dad's hand met my chin, and he eyed the small cut on the side of my face. He looked into my eyes, and I saw something flash in them. He pulled me close to him again as I cried.

"Not to worry, love. I'm here."

After a while I got dressed and we went downstairs, prepared to get breakfast. I was surprised that there weren't a plethora of photographers around. My dad was a particularly important businessman, owner of Hammond Industries in London, that supplied a great deal of materials to Australia and Africa, even to the America's.

"No entourage today?" I asked, trying to lighten the mood. He gave me a small sideways smirk, and I laughed. He always joked that Brits don't smile. My laughter, however, made that appear untrue as he smile slightly.

"No. I was able to slip away, I didn't even tell Marjory where I was going."

"The queen doesn't know where you are. For shame father," I exaggerated.

"What she doesn't know, won't hurt her and besides this is a private family matter." I was surprised to hear him say that. He always included her in everything. Maybe he was finally starting to realize what an awful person she was.

When we arrived at a small café on the other side of the city, I wasn't all too surprised when I saw Archie sitting at an outside table. I got out of the cab and walked up to him.

"You called my dad?" I hissed.

"Cousin, ye were attacked by a faceless assailant, shouldn't yer da ken?"

"I could have told him."

"Y'right."

"I would have." Archie rolled his eyes at me and then extended his hand to shake dad's as he appeared.

"Uncle."

"Nephew, it's good to see you."

"Guid ye see ye." Hearing the stark contrast between their accents was crazy.

"Shall we?" dad said as we took a seat at the table. I sat down and dad took a seat close to Archie, too close, where I suddenly felt that this wasn't just breakfast, this was an intervention of some sort. They both undid their silverware and put the cloth napkins in their laps, and I was suddenly staring at my grandfather as he always did the same thing.

I was not quite that proper, despite dad's insistence of my education being one of etiquette and poise. The idea made me laugh slightly; I was home schooled so I could travel with mom. Nothing very poised and proper of laying around in sweatpants and a hoodie, typing away, while waiting in an airport in Madrid.

"Lisey, we think you should go back to your mom's." The words caught me off guard, but I knew something was coming.

"I'm not giving up on this project."

"You were attacked and the man escaped. He recognized you. Don't you realize the peril this puts you in?" Dad asked.

"I'm fine." The truth was I knew that he was right. Despite doing everything to put space between my mother's fame and myself, it had finally been brought to light. I had no idea at what point he began following me, but if he recognized me there was a good chance that he knew where I was staying. He had run off, but that didn't mean he wouldn't be back. Anyone who knew about my mother, also knew about my father, they were both well off and I was their only child.

Kidnappings were really amped up when I was a kid, so mom always had extra detail when I was with her, and she tried her best to hide my face. There were very seldom photos throughout my life that connected us together. My name wasn't released to the public until after three years.

"For yer protection, it would be best to go back." Archie said. I shot daggers at him, I wouldn't be sitting here having this conversation with them right now, if he hadn't called my dad. I get it, he's my cousin and he was doing what he thought was right, trying to protect me, but I'm an adult and could have handled it myself.

"I'm staying. I appreciate and love you both for your concern, but I am a grown woman and will not quit this project. I need this for my future." Dad opened his mouth to protest. "Thank you for coming daddy. I love you and appreciate you coming all this way to help me, but I promise I'm fine. A little shaken as one would be, but I need to keep my commitment to this movie and the wonderful people I work with." He closed his mouth and nodded. My eyes were locked on him, so I couldn't help the jolt I felt shock my body as a hand touched mine. I turned to look at Archie.

"I daein you, cousin. We'se want yon to be safe." A small smile spread across my lips.

"I will be." I placed my hand on his, squeezing it gently. He smiled slightly and the conversation shifted to other matters, like the family in the highlands and dad's business ventures. It had been years since they had seen each other and even longer since the three of us were in the same place.

Chapter 32

Quinn

I kept looking at my phone, pulling up Lisey's contact, my thumb hovering over the call button each time before closing it again. I didn't want to bother her, but she never showed up on set today. Ludwig had been looking for her and Jafe had come asking as well.

"Lisey won't be coming to set today," I said as they joined me in my trailer.

"Is she okay?" Ludwig asked. I sighed heavily and cleared my throat.

"She was attacked last night."

"We should have been informed right away," Jafe said.

"It was late, I'm sure she's rather shaken as you can imagine."

"Was she injured?" Ludwig asked.

"No, she's alright." He released a sigh of relief and turned towards the door.

"You have my notes for the day; I'm going to check on her." Jafe nodded.

"I'll have something sent to her room. This has never happened before. I've had stars ambushed by fans but never had a crew member attacked randomly in the street," Jafe's stress was palpable, and I gently put my hands on his shoulders.

"She's not the type to make a big deal out of things, Jafe. If you would like to send her something small, that's fine, but she doesn't strike me as a grand gesture type of girl." He nodded and continued on his phone as he exited the trailer. I picked up my phone again.

"Fuck it." My fingers began typing when the screen disappeared as Barry was calling.

"What's up, Barry?" My tone clipped.

"Sheesh, catch you at a bad time?" I ran my hand down my face.

"No, just have a lot on my mind."

"Like what?" I huffed but told him everything that had happened.

"She did what?" Barry laughed boisterously on the other end of the phone, forcing me to hold it away from my face.

"Yeah, yeah. Yuck it up," I murmured.

"She actually got your one night stand a job as your assistant. That is some grade A Quinn bullshit right there, you have to marry this girl."

"I'm not getting married Barry, especially to her, she's crazy."

"She's perfect for you." His words stumped me. Thankfully, the door opened, and my elation melted when Ayda popped her head in.

"They need you on set, Quinn." I rolled my eyes.

"Barry, I'll call you back later." He laughed again and I hung up before he could even say goodbye. I didn't tell him about how Lisey had been attacked the night before. I wasn't sure how to even explain everything that happened after. I woke up, cradling her in my arms. She slept soundly through the night; she wasn't much of a roller or kicker which I was glad for. I anticipated she might have trouble staying asleep, but that didn't seem to be the case either. I had gotten up slowly, careful not to disturb her and left the room. Other than sleep we didn't do anything all night. I could faintly smell her shampoo aloft on the breeze as I exited the trailer.

***

That night as we got back to the hotel, I made a mad dash for Lisey's room. The elevator didn't seem to be running fast enough as my heart pounded in my chest. I wanted to make sure she was okay.

As the doors opened, I was stopped suddenly as the surprised wide eyes of my assistant stared at me.

"Where are you off to?" she asked.

"I'm going to check on Lisey." I eased myself past her. Her eyes on me as her lips poked out in a pout. I started down the hallway

"Do you love her?" I stopped.

"What would give you that crazy idea?" I asked spinning to look at her.

"You were distracted all day on set and now you are rushing off to see her."

"She's a coworker and what she went through wasn't something to be taken lightly."

"Sounds like you have feelings for her."

"I don't. I'm just making sure she's going to be alright to come to set tomorrow. We need her to help with the scenes." She rolled her eyes at me.

"Denial is a river, Quinn." I rolled my eyes at her and waved her off before leaving her in the hallway as I made my way to Lisey's room.

At the door, I knocked loudly. I shouldn't be here. After last night I should be as far away from her as possible.

The door opened and everything that was telling me to run quieted. Her eyes seemed lighter than yesterday as she looked up at me. Her face held more color than the night before.

"Can I help you, Quinn?" she asked. Her voice like satin cooling the hottest parts of me on a summer day.

"I just came to check on you."

"I'm alright." Our eyes were locked, I could stare into her emerald, green eyes forever. I shook my head and with a nod turned to walk away.

"Quinn." I stopped, turning to look at her.

"Yes?" Part of me hoped she would ask me to stay.

"Thank you," she said softly. I nodded and waited for her to say more, but nothing followed.

"Goodnight." She nodded and shut the door quietly.

I fell back into my bed with a humph. It seemed empty without her by my side as the phantom feeling of her in my arms crept its way into my memory. I exhaled with irritation, more at myself than anything else. I was letting her get to me and I didn't know why.

My phone began to ring, and I rolled over, grabbing it from the nightstand.

"Hey Barry," I sighed.

"Hey man, what's going on? Everything okay?"

"Yeah, just had a long day."

"Your ex-assistant or your current one?" he teased.

"Both."

"What did that brilliant girl do to you this time?"

"Nothing. It's what happened to her."

"What do you mean?"

"She was attacked last night while walking to the bar."

"Oh, shit. Is she okay?"

"For the most part."

"So, why is it bothering you so much?"

"Because I stayed the night with her."

"My dog, you finally got the girl in your bed?"

"Not exactly."

"What do you mean? You're Quinn Rose, there isn't a girl in a thousand miles that isn't dying to jump your bones."

"I stayed in her room, but we didn't do anything." He was quiet and I knew already what was coming next.

"That's not like you at all."

"I know."

"You're a playboy."

"I know."

"You're falling for her." I was quiet. The words floating in my head, like a gnat that I couldn't swat away.

"I can't fall for her. She isn't my type."

"She is your type, and you are falling for her."

"She's going to ruin everything we have worked for."

"How?"

"She doesn't strike me as the type that wants the limelight and that's all we have been chasing."

"Quinn, I'm going to give you some brotherly advice."

"Here we go," I sighed.

"You can have the best of both worlds. You can still have the band and the girl. You know that no matter what you do, I will support you, even if it means leaving all together."

"I can't just leave the band, Barry."

"But if she's the one you want to be with and that is the decision you come to, I'm behind you. We have been friends since we were kids, like brothers and seeing you happy is more important to me than going on tour. I love you man."

"Okay, now you are getting mushy."

"But it's true. You haven't been happy in a long time."

"That's not true, I'm happy with the band and with the tour. Look I'm even starring in a movie."

"Yeah, but I mean really happy. To have some-one in your life that makes you feel challenged and drives you crazy in the best ways." I ran my hand down my face. This was crazy, there was no way that I could have my cake and eat it to.

"I'm not going anywhere, Barry."

"Well, just think about what I said, Quinn. Somethings are just worth melting for." I snickered.

"Okay, Olaf." He laughed.

"Sorry, the girls and I were watching Frozen last night." My mind flickered to his family. Barry had a wife and two young daughters, Kyrie who was three and Ella who was one. He had a family and still balanced our crazy tour schedule.

"We should push the album back," I said.

"Why?"

"Because I want you to spend more time with your girls."

"Quinn, you know how it is, we have deadlines."

"Yeah, but family doesn't." He sighed on the other end of the phone, and I heard the distant sound of crying.

"That's my que."

"Alright, I'll talk to you tomorrow."

"Think about what I said."

"I will."

"Later, bud."

"Later." The call ended and I put the phone back down on the nightstand, before lacing my fingers together under my head, staring at the ceiling before I found sleep.

Chapter 33

Lisey

I shot up as the cool sensation of sweat flashed across my brow. My hands flew over my body as the disgusting feeling of that man's hands on me remained fresh from my nightmare. I immediately got out of bed. There was the slightest pitter patter of rain against the window as I walked towards it. Opening it, the breeze rushed in, followed by the drizzle, hitting my face. My mind was a frenzy. I had slept so well after everything happened and tonight I found myself distraught.

Closing the window, I headed to the armoire. I reached in and grabbed a cardigan, wrapping it around my shoulders before walking out in the hallway. The faint scent of home still lingering in the fibers. I had no idea where I was going, but I knew I had to get out of my room.

Before I could stop myself, I was knocking on the door of room six-thirty-three. I wrapped my arms around myself, hoping that it would go unanswered.

The door opened and Quinn stood looking at me. I expected that he would have been asleep by now, but instead he was wide awake.

"Lisey, what's wrong?"

"I couldn't sleep." There was an echo of thunder from outside.

"Did the storm wake you?"

"Not the one outside." He stepped aside.

"Come in." I nodded and stepped in through the door.

I took a seat on his bed, and he disappeared into the bathroom.

When he came out he was holding a glass of water. He handed it to me and with a trembling hand I took it and sipped it slowly. Lightning flashed and another boom of thunder followed. The gentle drizzle had turned into a downpour.

"Why did you come here?" I set the glass down on the nightstand.

"I don't know to be honest." He sat down next to me, and I could feel a heat radiating off his body.

"Are you okay?" His voice was quiet.

"I don't know." There was a tremble in my voice. He sighed softly.

"You can stay here tonight." It wasn't a question, and it wasn't a command. It was settled. I nodded. I slid my cardigan off my shoulders, and he took it. Standing he walked over to the desk and draped it over the chair, before returning to the bed. He laid down next to me and pulled the covers up over me, before settling against me his chest to my back and his arm around me. I twisted around underneath the weight of his arm so that I was facing him. His eyes were closed.

"Thank you," I whispered. He opened his eyes, and I felt drawn in. I slowly lifted my face towards his, carefully. His fingers gently touched my chin as his lips met mine. Slow at first, before it became a hungry kiss of desire. His fingers trailed down my neck, sending chills down my spine. Thunder cracked outside the window as I opened my mouth wider, letting his tongue slip inside as it danced around with mine.

He pulled away, heaving. Lightning lit up the room, and I could see his eyes on me.

"Don't stop," I whispered. His lips crashed against me once more and my hands found their way to his back, scratching my nails against his skin as a groan came from his chest. He pulled away.

"Lisey." My name sounded like music, coming from his lips. My mouth found his again and he rolled halfway on top of me, his hand caressing my face. I shifted underneath him, feeling him lift slightly as I peeled off my tank top. His hand caressing my breast as he took my mouth once more.

He pinched my nipple between his fingers, and a moan escaped me into his mouth. He began to trail kisses down my chin, along my neck until he reached my chest. Kneading one breast with his hand, he took the other in his mouth. Sucking and biting, sending me bucking up ever so slightly. I felt his hands slide down my body, to my waist, where he gently began to pull my shorts off.

"Quinn." I heard him chuckle as he began to move down my body, first with kisses, until he made it to my thigh. Nipping at the sensitive skin, a moan escaped me. He tossed my shorts to the floor.

His tongue found my clit, and he began flicking and sucking. His hands holding my hips down on the bed, so I couldn't take control. My upper back reeling with every delicious flick of his tongue. The pressure building up inside of me, made my breath quicken, until sweet release radiated through my entire body, sending a shiver shooting through me as I cried out his name.

"Quinn!"

Despite the tingling sensation in my body, he continued to lap up every bit of my excitement, my body shuddering in response.

He leaned back on his knees and smiled at me as he licked his lips. Lightning showing a glimmer of my juices left on his face. My chest heaved at the sight of him.

"Good girl," he whispered. His words sent a shockwave through me. I wanted more. It was almost as though he sensed it as well. He brought his face back up to mine and kissed me again, letting me taste myself.

"Do you want me to stop?" he whispered against my lips.

"No," I whispered back.

"Are you sure?" I nodded my head as my fingers found their way into his hair, and I kissed him hungrily. He pulled away gently and stood, dropping his boxers to the floor. His dick sprung out, hard, ready. I could feel a cool sweat break out across my brow; this man was going to ruin me. He got on his knees, spreading my legs open. He positioned himself and I could feel the head of his dick against my opening as he lubricated himself.

"Quinn." He stopped quickly.

"Do you want me to stop?" he asked.

"I've never done this before."

"We don't have to do this," he said.

"I want to. I just wanted you to know." It came out quiet as I was filled with embarrassment. He leaned into me again, his hard shaft sliding across my heat.

"I'll be gentle, I promise." I nodded. There was a slight tremble through my body as I felt his head at the opening. He pushed himself inside, stretching me and before I could utter a single cry, his mouth was on mine, taking it in. My body stretched as I took him all in, the pain lasting only for a minute, as he pulled out and slowly slid in again. He pulled away from me.

"Are you okay?" he asked. I nodded as a gasp escaped my lips. "Do you want me to stop?"

"No," I whispered. He kissed me again as he slowly pushed himself inside of me again. My fingers gripped his hair and pulling him towards me. A growl of urgency emanated from his chest and he began to pick up the pace. I broke the kiss as breathy moans escaped my lips.

"FUCK! You are so tight," he growled. He leaned back, grabbing my hips as he began to thrust harder, holding me in place to keep me from moving. Echoes of pleasure filled the room.

Before I knew it, he grabbed my arms and threw himself back on the bed, pulling me on top. Taking hold of my hips, he began to move underneath me, pulling me down to take all of him in.

Stretching me.

My body throbbing for more.

"Quinn!" I cried out as I felt myself explode around him. He didn't stop there, he kept going, thrusting harder and faster. My body was tired, and it took all I had to keep myself upright. His hand laced around my neck, and I felt a surge of excitement course through my veins. The pressure of his hand sent vibrations throughout my body, sending me quickly over the edge once more. He groaned loudly as he pulled me down, pushing himself as far in as he could go. A throbbing inside of me as he stopped and I collapsed on his chest. We were both covered in sweat, heaving as we laid there in the silence that followed. The only sound between us were the shuddered breaths left behind.

After a few minutes, he gently ran his fingers through my hair, wrapping them in my curls his lips crashed against mine. My body shook as he pulled himself out of me and gently rolled to his side, holding me against him. My head resting against his chest as I heard the pounding of his heartbeat.

CHAPTER 34

Quinn

My fingers trailed up and down her arm gently as she quietly snoozed at my side. It all made sense now. She was a virgin, that's why she panicked the way she had the first time. I felt like an asshole, treating her the way I had after, and I glanced down at her sleeping face. Whatever nightmares ailed her that led her to my room were at bay for the time being. My mind was racing almost as fast as my heart. Her delicate face seemed to glow in the pale light as the storm had passed and the moon had peeked out behind the clouds, illuminating her. I knew this girl was trouble. I knew it deep down that my flirting days were over.

So as I held her, I tried to quiet my mind. Finally, after what seemed like forever—I felt my eyelids grow heavier, and sleep claimed me fully.

As I woke the next morning, I was surprised to find Lisey had already left. I rolled over to grab my phone and found a steaming cup of coffee next to it. A smile formed in the corners of my mouth, and I pulled my phone from the charger. Opening it, there was a message from Lisey.

'Had to get to set early. Enjoy your coffee!'

My lips cracked as my smile widened. There was something different inside me. A new feeling. I launched myself out of bed. I wanted to get to set as fast as possible. Things were changing. I had spent so much time trying to get away from her, when really she was what I needed all along, more than just a fuck, she was so much more.

I threw the door open, and the paper was awaiting me as it always did. I picked it up, walking briskly down the hallway.

As I entered the elevator, I unwrapped the carefully folded newspaper to glimpse over the latest headlines. As I held it in full, my heart stopped. On the cover was a picture of Lisey and two men.

The headline: CEO David Hammond, spotted in Edinburgh with daughter Ellisia and friend."

My stomach dropped like I'd just missed a step in the dark.

My heart leapt into the back of my throat as I kept reading the story.

It mentioned her dad was the CEO and owner of Hammond Industries. How she was here working on an undisclosed project. The story continued on another page, and I quickly flipped to it. It was a picture of Lisey leaving The Balmoral Hotel. My heart fell into my stomach. They knew where she was staying and that meant so did that creep from the other night.

As the elevator doors opened, I was met by Ayda, as she held out a cup of coffee. The smile on her face dissipated as she realized I already had one in my hand.

"I'm sorry I should have brought you your coffee. You shouldn't have had to get it yourself," her voice was apologetic, but my mind was in a fury.

"Never mind that, we need to get to set. Now." She shuddered as the words came out with anger. Not only was I pissed about the story in the paper, but I was even more pissed that Lisey didn't tell me who she was. Ellisia Hammond, the name rang in my mind, the image of her bag at the airport.

How did I not connect the dots?

Not only was she the daughter of a multimillionaire CEO, but she was also the daughter of model Elenor Fitz.

The car pulled up to the set, and I immediately jumped out, leaving Ayda fumbling to get out of the backseat. My stride was direct.

"Good morning," Hardy said.

"Good morning." I said, my tone clipped. My eyes searched the large production area for Lisey, spotting her on a bench, poring over the script. I strode over to her, the heat in my eyes was pure as they met hers.

Her pouty lips broke into an innocent smile.

"Good mor." I slapped the paper down on the bench beside her, stopping her instantly. She looked down at the paper, taking it in her hands.

Her eyes widened as she read the headline.

"No," she whispered.

"Ellisia." Her eyes snapped to mine. "When were you going to tell me?"

"I don't understand why you're upset." There was a quiver in her voice.

"You didn't tell me who you were."

"Should it matter?"

"Yes it matters."

"Why?"

"You lied to me." I stalked back and forth within a foot of her. The rage blurring my vision.

Get control Q.

"I didn't lie to you. My name is Lisey Hammond."

"Daughter of CEO David Hammond and model Elenor Fitz." Her face stiffened as though I had just slapped her.

"So what? Does it really matter who my parents are?" She snapped, her eyes narrowing at me.

"You're practically famous."

Just like that I felt small again, the kid who couch hopped in L.A., scraping by with nothing more than a guitar and a dream.

"I'm not nearly famous."

"As the only daughter of two famous people you are practically paparazzi royalty."

"Why does that matter to you? I'm trying to hide from their limelight, not live in it."

"You are here working on this production for what? Can't you go anywhere and have everything handed to you? You probably never had to work for a damn thing." The words came out of me faster than I could stop them.

I had clawed from the gutters to be here, and she was here purely because she was bored.

Her eyes fell.

"I worked hard to be here."

I scoffed.

"Bullshit. You wouldn't know what arduous work was if it hit you in your pretty little model face." She stiffened.

"You don't know what I went through to."

"It must have been so hard," I interrupted, sarcasm laced in every word. My chest heaved as we stared at each other silently. She rose from the bench instantly. I thought she was going to slap me and part of me wished she would. Instead, her eyes crinkled, and tears began to wash down her face as she shoved the paper back into my chest before disappearing down the road. Angrily, I crumpled the paper and tossed it in the bin.

I didn't see her on set for the rest of the day. Ludwig was advising on shots, chatting with Hardy and Jafe in between takes. It was a good day for us to be filming a fighting scene.

I was pissed.

"Action!" I stepped to my left a few paces, hands up ready to fly. When Branigan stepped toward me I jabbed, before dodging a blow from the right. I jumped back, as he attempted another strike, the air barely whistling against my face. I jumped forward landing a hit against his cheek, he stumbled back. He raised his glove to his face as his shoulders fell.

"Cut!" Hardy's voice held irritation this was the third time, I had landed a hit on Branigan, when we weren't actually supposed to hit each other. I watched as he spit the mouthguard out.

"Dude, what the hell?" I sighed heavily as I dropped my stance.

"I'm sorry."

"That's the third time. You keep it up and we will really be fighting." The anger in his voice was understandable. I felt footsteps making the box bounce as they came towards me. I turned to see Jafe standing in front of me, his thumb and forefinger pressed to the bridge of his nose.

"What's going on with you?" he asked.

"I'm having an off day." He sighed heavily.

"I need you to get out of your head and into your character's." He clapped his hands together.

"Shift it!" Hardy's voice echoed over the set. I looked around as everyone began to scramble. Jafe sighed again.

"Get your shit together, kid. We are going to move on to another scene." I nodded and he walked away.

As I walked into my trailer, I was beating myself up. I had to get my fight with Lisey out of my head. I grabbed a bottle of scotch from on top of the mini fridge and poured myself a shot. This would help calm me and get me ready for the next scene.

***

As I opened the door to the club, the music was loud, and I felt the thrumming of the music radiate through my body. There were men sitting around at tables, whooping, and laughing as the beautiful girl danced around on the pole before them. Her hair was blonde; her skin was bare except for the lacey thong she was wearing. I took a seat at a table in the back and waited for the show to end.

As her set ended and she disappeared off the stage, I took that as my chance. I slipped in the back and found my way weaving down the hallway, until I came to a door that had a star on the front. I knocked lightly.

"Just a minute," she called. Her voice radiating every bit of sweetness it once held so long ago. The door opened and I looked at her. The blonde wig now gone, giving way to her jet-black tresses. Her eyes wide.

"Ayaan?"

"Cut!" The bell rang and I let out a sigh. Jafe walked up to me and Marina.

"That was a perfect take you two. Well done. Take an hour for lunch and we will be back here then to do the next scene." I nodded. As he walked away I felt Marina's eyes on me.

"What?"

"Have lunch with me." I nodded and she closed the door behind her as she walked away.

I waited briefly outside her trailer for her to be ready. When she came out she was still wearing the makeup from the shot but now had on a hoodie and sweatpants.

"You sure can dress down, huh?" I asked with a laugh.

"Hey, I can't be fishnets and black leather all the time."

We settled down at the café just outside of the set. We placed our orders quickly.

As a beer appeared in front of me I took a swig before quietly waiting for her to speak.

"What's going on, Quinn?"

"What do you mean?"

"You've been off all day."

"It's nothing."

"I saw you get into a little spat with Lisey earlier. Does it have something to do with that?" I looked at her before taking another drink of my beer.

"It was nothing."

"Doesn't seem to be nothing, if you are stewing over it hours later." She leaned back in her chair, reading me like a book.

"I'll get over it."

"What happened?"

"She lied to me."

"About what?"

"Who she was."

"How?"

"She's got famous parents, and she didn't tell me about them."

"So, because she didn't say who her parents were, makes her a liar?"

"No. It's the fact she didn't tell me who she really was."

"And who is that?"

"Ellisia Hammond."

"Who did she say she was?"

"Lisey Hammond."

"So how did she lie?" I took another swill of my beer and looked at her.

"She's a nepo baby."

"And that bothers you?"

"I worked hard to be here. I climbed out of the gutters of Los Angeles to be where I am today, I had nothing handed to me."

"And she did."

"She probably grew up with a silver spoon in her mouth," I spat.

"Why would a nepo baby be working at a production company as a low-level screenwriter, if she could have anything she wanted?"

"Probably for laughs," I scoffed. She leaned over and slapped my arm.

"Get out of your head, idiot." Her response shocked me. "My parents are famous. I worked hard to be where I am without their help." I stared at her.

"Who are your parents?"

"Bleigh and Morvi Korkovski."

"Deputy Korkovski of Moldova?"

"One of the deputies of parliament, yes, and my mother is an advisor to the president." I suddenly felt stupid.

"What do they think about you living in America and being in a band."

"They didn't care so much about that. What they cared about was when they found out that I was married to a woman."

"You have a wife?"

"Yes, Iliana."

"I didn't know you were married."

"Few people do. My wife likes her privacy, so she doesn't exactly come on tour or go to shows that often." A light lit up inside my head.

"So, you can have it all." It came out like a whisper.

"What do you mean?"

"I've been fighting myself, between having what I want and having what I worked for."

"What is it you want, Quinn?" My eyes met hers and in them I could see that she already knew. I wanted Lisey, I wanted her to be a part of my life, today, tomorrow, forever. "Then go get her."

CHAPTER 35

Lisey

"Lis, you worked too hard to give up now."

"I know, Aggie, but I have to get out of here."

"Why?"

"There was an article in the paper about my dad and me. There was a picture and now Quinn is pissed off at me."

"Why does it matter if he's mad." I dropped my head to the side, looking at her through the screen as the tears began to seep down my face.

"Oh, Lisey," she sighed.

"I slept with him."

"Oh, honey."

"It's even worse than that."

"What do you mean?"

"I'm falling for him."

"Then why are you running away?"

"Because according to him, I'm a nepo baby who has never had to work for anything. He hates me."

"Lisey, he was probably just upset."

"It doesn't matter; the things he said to me were unfair and cruel."

"Maybe he will come around."

"So, I should just what? Forgive him?" She was silent.

"Lisey, you don't have to quit the production."

"Yes, I do."

"But you need this for the future you are trying to build."

"What I need is to get away from him."

"I hate to see you this way." I stopped stuffing the clothes into my bag and sighed, leaning my head back to stare at the ceiling. Everything I had ever done had led me to this moment and I had worked so hard to get here. Now I was going to throw it all away to escape the feelings that were growing inside of me.

"I love him, Aggie." The words came from my lips as a whimper.

"Then you should stay."

"I can't. I already told Hardy and Lou that I quit."

"And they just let you?"

"No, they told me to take a few days to think about it and let them know. They want me to stay. Lou really wants me to stay. He says I have a vision he hasn't experienced in a long time."

"Then you should stay."

"I need time. I need to put distance between myself and Quinn."

"Where are you going to go?"

"I was thinking about staying with Archie for a few days, but I don't think that will be far enough, as he lives here in the city."

"So where are you going then?"

"My dad's in London." I heard her clacking away on her computer.

"I can get a flight and be their first thing in the morning."

"You don't have to come."

"Yes, I do. You are my best friend, and you are heartbroken. I need to be there for you." More tears began to stream down my face.

"Are you sure?"

"Hell yeah." I heard her clicking away again. The sound of her mouse moving along as her nails hit the keyboard.

It wasn't long before she spoke again.

"All booked, I'll see you at eight in the morning in London."

"I'll come to meet you; I can have dad send a car."

"Sounds good, I better get packing, I have to leave for the airport shortly."

"Thank you, Aggie."

"Chin up. You're a bad bitch, remember that." I laughed slightly.

"I love you."

"I love you too. I'll see you first thing." I nodded and the call ended.

I finished packing my bag and practically had to sit on it to get it to close.

As I walked out into the hallway, I felt a twitch of guilt starting in my stomach. Quinn's words echoed in the back of my brain, and I wanted to call him and give him a piece of my mind. I held my phone in my hand, ready to make the call, but thought better of it. Turning the sound off, I opened my carryon and stuffed it deep down inside.

As I got on the elevator a single tear slipped down my cheek. I brushed it away, avoiding making eye contact with an elegant older woman who shared the ride down to the lobby with me.

As the doors opened, I let her walk out first. The clerk behind the desk nodded at me as I approached.

"Good afternoon, Miss Hammond."

"I'll be leaving for a few days. I won't require any room services until my return." He nodded.

"Very good, miss. I'll be sure to leave a note for our staff." I nodded and headed towards the door.

Outside, the clouds had gathered, and it had started to rain. It was a good thing it started when it did, they might wrap early today, and I wanted to be as far away as possible before Quinn came back. Should I run into him, I might not leave at all.

"You're a nepo baby." The words he spat towards me settled in my head again, making my stomach do back flips.

The honk of a horn broke me from my thoughts, and I dragged my bag down the stairs. I was met at the bottom by the driver of the car, he held the door open, nodding at me as I got in. He shut the door, and I watched as he picked up my bag and threw it into the back of the car. As he climbed in, he pulled back out into the dreary street.

"Where to miss?" he asked.

"The airport please." He nodded and I leaned back against the seat, letting my head rest on the cool glass of the window.

As the argument with Quinn clouded my thoughts, I wasn't paying attention until the car came to a sudden stop. I sat up and looked around. We were in a parking lot.

"What's wrong?" I asked.

"Flat tire, miss." I looked out the window; it was pouring outside. "I'll just be a minute to fix it."

"But it's pouring, you'll catch your death out there."

"Not to worry miss." He got out of the driver's seat, and I leaned against the back door.

The door flew open so fast that I practically fell out of the car, his hands grabbed me, pulling me out. I landed on the soaked ground, my jeans soaking up the puddle underneath me. I began reeling, as his grip tightened on me.

"Help!" My shrill scream echoed into the gloomy abyss, as I realized we were nowhere near people. His hand tightly wrapped around my mouth and nose with a cloth, and the world began to fade. I continued to flail against him, trying to fight him off.

"Don't worry, Miss Hammond." His voice changed and I recognized it. It was him.

My eyes fluttered as I tried to commit his face to memory. Dark hair, icy blue eyes, a tattoo on his neck and a scar that ran over his top lip. My body began to still as everything began to blur.

"I'll take good care of you Ellisia." It came out as a snarl and he grinned, pleased with himself as the rain pelted us, drenching me as the world went black.

CHAPTER 36

Quinn

We wrapped early due to inclement weather. Although most of our shots were inside, they were calling for flooding, which would make it impossible to get back to the city.

The car seemed as though it wasn't going fast enough as anxiety ran through me. I never saw Lisey again on set and I had to talk to her. I had to apologize for being the world's biggest asshole. It didn't matter to me who her parents were, she was Lisey, and I was completely in love with her.

The car had barely come to a stop before I was leaping out of the backseat.

"Quinn, slow down!" Ayda chirped behind me. I wasn't letting up. I was wrong and I had to make sure that Lisey knew it. I was going to tell her. I was a fool to think I needed to get away from her, when she was everything I needed all along. I was going to do whatever I had to, to make it right.

I bound through the lobby, my feet slipping on the polished floor as my sopping feet pounded against it towards the elevator. The doors opened and I nearly crashed into an older couple making their way out.

"Sorry." I said quickly as I leapt in and began mashing the button for the third floor.

"Slow down, you're going to hurt someone."

"I'm sorry, but I'm in love with a girl and I have to tell her." I saw a glimmer in the older gentleman's eye as he looked at his wife and nodded. The doors closed and the elevator began the agonizingly slow ascent to Lisey's floor.

As the door opened, I rushed out and down the hallway, turning the corner quickly, I halted as I saw Archie standing at the door. He was leaning against it. His eyes met mine and I could see anger in them. He strode up to me, stopping within a few inches of my face. I felt anger boiling up inside of me.

"What are ye doing here?"

"What are you doing here?"

"Scannin up."

"For what?"

"Lisey," he hissed. The urge to beat this pompous asshole with my fist was growing.

"For the record, she was in my bed last night, not yours, so you might want to scan someone else." He crinkled his nose in disgust.

"You're quite the dobber, aren't ye?"

"What the fuck does that mean?"

"Idiot, fool, whatever you American's like to call it," he spat. I grabbed his pressed white shirt and raised my fist. He remained completely unphased.

"You can ask her yourself, you Scottish bastard."

"I dinnae ken nor care who she is fucking."

"Then why are you hanging around so much?" The words came out seething. He put his hands up on my shoulders and pushed me away as I kept my balled fist raised.

"She's my scunne."

"What does that mean?" He ran his hand over his face and sighed.

"My cousin." I dropped my fist and stared at him.

"She's your cousin?"

"Aye." Suddenly I felt relief fill me. Here this whole time when I would see them together, I thought he was seeing her, when in fact they were family. I brushed my hand down the front of my shirt.

"I'm sorry." I offered my hand to him, and he reluctantly shook it.

"Ken, where she is?" he asked.

"I haven't seen her on set all day, except for earlier." The harsh words I said to her began to play in my mind and I wanted to hit my head against the wall. God I was such a fucking idiot.

"I knocked on the door, but she dinnae answer." I walked past him lightly and went to the door. I knocked as he joined me.

"Lisey?" I waited patiently, listening intently for any movement inside, but there was nothing.

"I don't know where else she would have gone."

"I tried to call her, but no answer." I pulled my phone from my pocket and pulled up her contact. I hit the button and listened to it as it rang.

"Hi, you've reached Lisey, I can't come to the phone right now, but." I ended the call.

"Her phone's on."

"I wonder where she could be."

"Maybe she's at the bar with Owen."

"Tiugainin." He began walking down the hallway. I had no idea what he said, but I followed him.

***

"Owen, whaur ye fae?" Archie hollered as we entered the bar. Owen came out behind the bar from the back.

"Whit like are ye?"

"Has Lisey been here today?" I asked, the urgency in my voice evident.

"No. I haven't seen her." I leaned against the bar.

"Where could she be?" Owen placed a pint in front of me, and I took a seat. He then handed the paper to Archie.

"Did you read the paper?" Archie grabbed the paper up; it rustled in his hands as he held it. His eyes scanned the story, before he dropped the paper down.

"Fucking cunts, they dinnae ken how to leave people be." He sat down on the stool next to me and Owen put a pint in front of him as well.

"Why are you looking for her?" I looked at Archie; he never did tell me why he was looking for Lisey.

"She left me a message, she was upset, with this fucker over here." He nodded in my direction. I felt a small smile crease into the corner of my lips and a slight chuckle. She was pissed at me and rightfully so, but hearing his accent with the word fucker, just make me laugh a little bit.

"It's no funny."

After we finished our pints, Archie paid Owen, and we stepped back out into the rainy day.

"Here's my card, give me a ring if ye hear anything." I nodded.

"I'll send you a text so you have my number, that way if you hear anything you can let me know as well."

"Aye." We shook hands and he walked off down the street to his car, while I rushed back to the hotel.

As my shoes squeaked across the polished floor, I made my way to the desk. The clerk looked as though the sound was making him grind his teeth, so I wiped my shoes on the mat in front of the desk.

"How can I help you, Mr. Rose?" he asked.

"I'm looking for Miss Hammond, have you seen her today?" He turned to the computer and began to tap the keyboard.

"Miss Hammond is out."

"What do you mean out?"

"I have a note in my system that says she would be returning in a few days and didn't require turn-down services." I felt my heart drop into my stomach and nodded.

"Thank you." I walked away from the counter and pulled my phone out to text Archie.

CHAPTER 37

Lisey

My head was foggy as I opened my eyes. Everything was dimly lit, and I couldn't remember what had happened.

"Good evening, Miss Hammond." That voice. Startled, I shot up and found myself backing against a wall. I was sitting on a bed, and he was sitting in a chair at the edge.

"What do you want?"

"Just to talk."

"I have nothing to say to you." He pulled a knife out and flicked it open, letting it dance in his hand. I could feel the small nick on my cheek that had since healed begin to burn from the memory.

"How much do you think your parents would pay to get you back?"

"I don't know why you think my parents would have any money to pay you." He laughed. He pulled a newspaper from behind his back and tossed it down in front of me. I tried to edge closer to look at it, but the sudden tug and clinking sound stopped me. I turned my head to see that my wrists were bound in shackles, chained to the wall. I looked back down at the paper, and there was the story. My picture right there in black and white. I looked up at him and he stood, approaching me quickly, he grabbed my face before I could move away.

"Tell me love."

"I don't know," my voice shook. I felt the knife on my face as he trailed it slowly down my skin, I could tell it was the back of the blade, because if it weren't he would have cut me wide open.

"I'm sure Ms. Fitz and Mr. Hammond would pay a great deal of money for their only daughter's life."

"Who are you?" I had to know. This couldn't just be some weird fan fantasy or quick scheme, he had to have ties to my family somehow, no one was this desperate. He stopped the knife at my collar bone and snickered.

"No need to worry about that," he laughed. He pulled the knife away and then ran his calloused finger over my cheek, making my skin crawl. With hands like that he had to be a working man, but what kind of work, I wasn't sure I wanted to know.

"Please, let me go," I pled.

"I can't collect if I don't have you here with me. Besides, we could have some fun together, while we wait." The way he said that made my stomach flip. He stepped away, thumbing the tip of the blade, the sharp edge pinging off his skin.

"Why are you doing this?"

"Because I can."

"That's not an answer." He rushed me again, pressing the sharp part of the blade against my neck, just off to the side of my throat. I could feel the pinching feeling as it began to break the skin.

"I'm going to get what is owed to me!" He yelled. Tears flooded my eyes and began to seep down my face as I shook. He pressed the blade a little harder and I bit back, trying to keep from crying out. He pulled away from me, and I let out a heavy sigh as tears continued down my face. He sat down in the chair again, once more playing with the blade. He held it firmly in his hand and pointed it at me.

"I think I could get a cool two million off your folks." I remained quiet as I shook my head. I tilted my head towards my chained hands, fisting away the tears, so I could see him clearer, so I could capture his entire face in my memory for later, so I could describe him to the police.

"If you are ever taken, don't look them in the face." I heard my mother's voice. I was about eleven at the time.

"Why not?" I had asked.

"Because your survival depends on it, if you don't see their face, you can't tell the police who did it. If you look at them, they will kill you." Her words reverberated in my ears as I looked at him. This wasn't going to end with me going home. As the realization hit me, there was a wicked smile that spread across his face. He already knew the moment he took me what he was going to do. Use me for ransom and once he got the money, I was a goner. I breath hitched in my chest as he stood again.

"Sleep well, Ellisia. Tomorrow the work begins." He headed for the door.

"Please, don't do this." His back remained turned. He opened the door and slammed it shut behind him. "Let me go!" I screamed. It echoed out into and down the hallway for what seemed like forever. I looked around the room as the dim light began to fade with the oncoming night.

CHAPTER 38

Quinn

I sat in the hotel bar, my fingers dancing around the rim of the rocks glass in front of me. I had tried to call her several times with no answer. The last time I had called, it went straight to voicemail, either it had died, or she was ignoring me.

"Why the long face, Quinn?" The voice startled me, and I looked up to see Ludwig as he took a seat next to me.

"It's just my face," I replied as I brought the glass to my lips again.

"You look like a man with a broken heart." I stiffened, as I put the glass back down.

"That obvious, huh?" He chuckled slightly before taking the glass of wine that had been set before him in his hand.

"You aren't hiding it well at all, boy." He took a sip.

"I just can't help but feel something is off. I have no idea where she is, she won't answer my calls."

"All you know is why she left." His words struck me.

"I was a dick," I confessed.

"She quit the movie," he sighed.

"What?"

"She said she wanted to quit and go back home. I begged her, hell even Hardy begged her and that man doesn't know what begging is."

"So, she went back to LA?"

"No, Mage offered her a few days off to think about it, and she agreed. I believe she said she was going to see her father."

"So, she flew to London." I felt something ignite in my chest.

"Yes." I pulled my phone from my pocket and started searching flights. The next one was leaving around eleven in the morning. I punched in my information and bought the ticket.

"I'm going to fly over there tomorrow."

"But we have work to do."

"Are there any shots you guys can film around me?" He smiled slightly.

"Perhaps."

"Great, I'll let him know then. I shouldn't be gone longer than a day and then we will come back and finish the movie."

"How will you ever find her?"

"I have her cousin's number; he's bound to know where his uncle lives." I finished the drink in front of me and stood.

"Go get her, boy." There was a twinkle in his eyes and a gentleness to his words.

"I will."

I walked down the hall of the fifth floor, stopping at the room number five oh four. I knocked loudly on the door.

Almost instantly the door flew open and in front of me stood Ayda, a mask on her face and her hair in a towel.

"Mr. Rose!" She began to peeled the mask off and remove the towel from her head.

"I'm flying to London tomorrow; you can have the day to do as you please." She seemed taken aback by the words that had just come from my mouth.

"When should I expect you back?"

"The following day, but if things change I'll call you."

"Thank you," she said softly. I pulled some notes from my pocket.

"Here, go see your family in Glasgow, that should be enough for a round-trip ticket and lunch." She gently took the bills from me and nodded her head.

"This isn't necessary." She said, as she tried to hand it back to me. I took her hand and closed her hand around it.

"Go and enjoy yourself, you've worked hard for me, let me do this for you." She nodded and closed the door as I headed up to my room to pack.

The phone rang several times before connecting.

"Hey bro, what's up." Barry's voice was loud as it came through from the other end.

"I love you and hate you at the same time," I said as I held the phone to my ear.

"What did I do now?" Barry asked.

"You were right you smug bastard."

"Oh, I was? Are you really that surprised?"

"You know me even when I don't, Barry."

"What are you going to do now?"

"Right now, I'm packing my shit."

"Are you coming home?"

"No, I'm going to get my girl."

"Where is she?"

"I was a total dick, Barry. She tried to quit, and they wouldn't let her. They asked her to take a few days to think about it, so she flew over to see her dad in London."

"So, you're going to London to do what exactly."

"Grovel. Beg. Apologize, do whatever I have to, to get her back on the set to finish this movie."

"What about after."

"Turns out you were right about that to."

"Meaning?"

"I can have it all. I can have the rockstar life and the girl."

"Hopefully, you don't mean the old rockstar life."

"Fuck that, my fuck roulette days are over, she's the one Barry. I can feel it, in every fiber and nerve of my being."

"It's about time."

"What do you mean?"

"You've been closed off for years, screwing this chick, that chick and the like, but never really finding that one person that changed you. You have seemed different since you met her on that plane."

"I feel even more different now that I'm not running from the feelings."

"Does she love you back?"

"I don't know."

"Did you tell her you loved her?"

"No."

"Are you going to tell her when you see her?"

"That's the plan." I stuffed my shit into a bag and zipped it closed.

"I'll give you a call tomorrow when I get to London, I have to get some sleep."

"Alright buddy, let me know when you make it."

"I will." I ended the call and tossed my bag down next to the door. Throwing my clothes off I crawled into bed, calling her one last time. Again, it went to voicemail and an iron grip clinched around my heart. I just hoped it wasn't too late.

CHAPTER 39

Lisey

My eyes were filled with sleep as the sun rose through the tinted window of the room. I hadn't slept all night, afraid of what that lunatic might do if he caught me sleeping off guard. My lips were dry as I licked them. I hadn't had anything to eat or drink since before I left the hotel that morning. Whenever that was. I had no idea how long I had been out. I heard a door creak open down the hallway and my body shuddered as anticipation filled the room.

As the door opened, he stalked in with a tray. There was a glass of water and some broken pieces of bread. My hands were still chained to the wall as he sat it down in front of me. He pulled the chair close.

"I have to keep you chained up, little bird. I don't want you to fly away, now." He picked up a piece of bread and held it out to my lips. I kept them closed. I wasn't a child and refused to be belittled this way. If I were going to eat I would feed myself.

"Go on," he prodded. My lips formed a hard straight line. He smashed the mealy loaf against them, and I turned my head away. He growled as he threw it down on the platter and grabbed the water, pushing the glass to my lips. Again, my mouth remained closed, despite the desperation I felt burning in my body for the cool liquid, I refused to yield. He tried to shove the glass into my lips again and I turned my head. Angry he took a step back, grabbing my chin forcefully with one hand he tilted my head back and poured the water on my face. The icy water went into my nose, forcing me to open my mouth to breath, he moved the glass as some water fell into my mouth, before forcing a piece of bread inside, practically shoving it down my throat. He released my face, and I threw my head down, trying to spit out the hunk of bread to keep it from becoming stuck and choking me. He picked up a paper he had on the tray and stuck me with it across the face several times.

"Didn't anyone ever teach you that it's rude to turn down someone's offer of food?" His voice was laced with venom, but I could smell the strong, acrid stench of whiskey on his breath. He opened the paper and tossed it down in front of my feet. I whimpered as he turned away from me, pulling something from his front pocket. He spun around and I shrank away. He had his phone in hand, pointed at me. He looked over the top if it at me and sighed.

"This won't work." He walked towards me and without recoil, hit me across the face. I sat there stunned as he stood back. The sting from his open palm on my face brought tears to my eyes, but yet he seemed unsatisfied.

"Sorry, love."

He balled his fist, and I flinched as he drove it towards me.

The force of the blow hitting my cheek, knocked my head against the brick wall I was leaning against, dazing me further.

I tried to see straight but everything was spinning.

He looked at me again.

"Needs little more oomph."

He took his open palm and smacked straight down on my nose.

He wasn't trying to break it and possibly stab my brain, he was trying to get his point across, and on my end it was working, as blood began to gush down from my nose and into my lap.

He stood back again and grinned as I looked up at him through my lashes, as I kept my head forward, letting the blood seep into my jeans.

He stood back again and used his thumbs and forefingers to form a square as though he was lining up his shot. He smiled seeming happy with the angle and picked his phone up from the chair.

"Smile big for your daddy." I looked up at him, and the flash blinded me. He looked at the photo, nodding in amusement before turning it to me.

"Look at you there, my little bird. Pretty as a picture." My hair was disheveled, and I was covered in blood, with the strong hint of a bruise forming on my cheek where he had hit me. He turned the phone away again and looked at it again.

"This picture makes me hard as fuck," he groaned. Blood had seeped into my mouth, and I spat it at him. He rushed towards me, grabbing my face in his hand and forcing his lips on mine, trying to get my mouth to open. As he managed to wedge his tongue in ever so slightly, I bit down, forcing him to draw back. He landed a back hand against my face, and I fell flat on the bed, my head spinning as the blood began to seep into the mattress under me.

"You'll pay for that you little bitch." He snarled and then stormed out of the room. My head throbbed, but I wasn't sure if it was from the loss of blood or the smack to the wall that had been second hand to the initial hit. My eyes began to slowly close. All I wanted right now was to go to sleep, but I was afraid of what might happen once my eyes closed. As the room began to fade, I saw Quinn's face. Despite how badly he treated me, I still longed for his embrace. To tell him how I felt, because right now, there was no telling if I would ever get the chance.

CHAPTER 40

Quinn

The car pulled up to the curb, and I got out quickly, grabbing my bag and slinging it over my shoulder.

As I walked in I headed straight for security, I had my boarding pass on my phone. I had tried to call Lisey several times when I got up and on my way here, but there was no answer. Luckily, I had gotten the address for her dad's place from Archie.

"Be wary," he warned.

"Of what, her dad?"

"No, her stepmum. She's a nasty old thing."

"Noted."

I pulled my phone from my pocket and decided to send her a text. I was walking not paying any attention to where I was going when I felt hands on my chest. I looked up and was staring down into the dark fiery brown eyes of young woman.

"Pardon me miss," I said.

"Where is she, shitbag?" Her words caught me off guard and I wasn't sure how to respond. Her grip on my shirt tightened as she shook me.

"Who are you talking about?"

"My daughter Ellisia Hammond," a commanding voice said from behind her. I looked passed her and striding toward me was David Hammond himself.

"I was just on my way to London to find her, sir."

"Cut the act, asshole, where is she?" I knew right away that this girl was straight out of Los Angeles. I gently put my hands on her wrists, pleading with my eyes for her to let me go. She relented, yanking her hands free of my shirt, wiping them on her legs like I was diseased.

"Really, I'm on my way to find her now."

"No bother, my daughter never arrived in London." His words hit me like a ton of bricks.

"What do you mean she never arrived?"

"I was supposed to meet her there this morning and she never came. I called her mom who called her dad, and he said she never made it."

"I don't understand," I stammered.

"I was told by Mr. Ludwig that she had gone to visit her father."

"Well, she never made it," the woman snapped. My heart began pounding in my chest. What had happened? I opened my contacts and found Archie's number right away. He answered on the first ring.

"Quinn?"

"Lisey's missing."

"What are ye saying?"

"I'm at the airport and just ran into her dad and her," I looked at the girl who was glaring at me, "her friend. They said she never made it to London."

"I'm nearby, I'll come for ye. Hang tight."

"Alright." The call ended and I turned my eyes back to the woman glaring at me.

"I promise you I have no idea where she is."

"You better hope she isn't hurt, because if she is." She stopped as tears filled her eyes.

"Aggie," Mr Hammond said softly.

"No, if he wouldn't have been such a dick, then she wouldn't have left to go to London." I felt my shoulders sag. She was right.

"I was a complete asshole, Aggie. But I promise I will do whatever it takes to help find her. I was going to London to tell her how I felt, because I was wrong and I love her." Her eyes softened slightly.

"Good." Her tone was clipped, but there wasn't time for that conversation.

"Come on, Archie is on his way to get us now."

***

When Archie arrived, Mr. Hammond slid into the front seat while Aggie and I got into the back.

"Has anyone talked to her?" Archie asked.

"No, her phone has been going to voicemail for me all day. I thought she was just pissed off at me," I said.

"I haven't been able to get ahold of her either," Aggie replied. Over the shoulder of the passenger seat, I could see Mr. Hammond on his phone. It was none of my business, so I leaned back, my mind racing with questions.

"Oh my God." Mr. Hammond's voice broke the short-lived silence.

"What is it, uncle?" Archie asked. Mr. Hammond held up his phone and there was a picture of Lisey. Blood was running down her face, and a bruise was forming on her cheek. There was a newspaper sitting at her feet with today's headline.

"Good morning, Mr. Hammond as you see I have your lovely daughter here with me today. I am demanding two million pounds for her safe return. You have until four o'clock this evening to respond with a picture of the money in exchange for a location. No cops or your precious little girl will be dead before dinner."

My blood ran cold as he finished reading. That's why she wasn't answering her phone and had never made it to London, there was a good chance she never even made it to the airport.

"What do we do?" Archie asked.

"We drop these kids off at the Balmoral Hotel and then you and I are going to the bank."

"You can't seriously be thinking about paying this psycho," I said leaning forward from the backseat.

"He has my daughter. I don't care what the cost is. I'd give him five million for her safe return. She is my only child, and her life is priceless to me." I grew quiet and leaned back. I felt a shudder next to me and looked over at Aggie who was silently weeping as she leaned against the window. I knew she hated me right now, but I was scared too. I put my arm around her shoulders and pulled her into a hug.

"We are going to get her back," I whispered. She nodded against me gently, as we headed back to the hotel in silence.

As Archie pulled up outside the Balmoral I got out on the street side and walked around to open the door for Aggie. Mr. Hammond rolled down his window.

"Not a word of this to anyone. The wrong people catch wind of this and Lisey will." He stopped. I nodded my head. I didn't need him to say the thing we feared the most. He began to put the window up.

"Mr. Hammond." He stopped and looked at me briefly.

"I want to go with you for the exchange."

"There's too much at stake."

"Please, sir. I'm not the greatest man, but I love your daughter. I want to ensure she is returned safely." He looked at me with a glare before nodding.

"We'll be in touch." The window rolled up, and they took off down the street. I gently took Aggie by the elbow and led her inside.

Ayda was on her way out the door as we walked in.

"Mr. Rose, I thought you had left for London."

"Change of plans," I replied.

"Do you need me to stay?"

"No, go see your family Ayda." She looked from me to Aggie and nodded before she disappeared through the door. Aggie stifled a laugh.

"What's so funny?" I asked.

"I heard all about Lisey getting her hired as your assistant." She turned her head to look out the door where Ayda had just disappeared. "She's cute."

"Yeah, yeah, it was so funny." She started laughing slightly, but only briefly before the laughter turned to tears.

"It's going to be okay," I whispered.

"It has to be, she's my best friend." I rubbed her arm as I gently guided her into the bar.

Chapter 41

Lisey

As I opened my eyes my head was throbbing. I had no idea what time it was, but I was just grateful that when I woke up, he wasn't in the room. The paper was still lying on the bed. Dragging myself up, I tried to scan it as much as possible to get some sort of idea of how much time had passed, at least to know what day it might be. The chains rattled as I pulled trying to get a good look.

The sound of a door creaking open echoed down the hallway, and I felt my heart begin to pound in my chest. Who knew what this crazy asshole had in store for me next. Maybe he was coming to kill me, maybe he was coming to do something far worse.

He stumbled into the door; a smile plastered on his face as he came towards me. He didn't have to be too close for me to tell he was drunk off his ass. The stench that came from him was strong. I turned my head as he put his hands on either side of me, leaning down, eyeing me up and down. His beady eyes making my skin crawl as they scanned over me. He leaned in and sniffed my hair, making my stomach turn.

"Your daddy has agreed on a price."

"What?" He stumbled back and smiled.

"We have a deal. Two million pounds for his precious little girl."

"Why did you go after my father?" I asked. He snickered as he held a finger up and wagged it at me.

"Now, now. Don't think that a little whiskey in my blood is going to give you all the answers."

"Well does it really matter?" He stumbled slightly as he cocked his head in question. "I know how this works. I'm never going to see my family again."

"Why do you say that?"

"Because I've seen your face," I whispered. He laughed and clapped his hands.

"You really are a smart girl, Ellisia. Bravo." He clapped his hands close to my face, making me wince. He reached out then and gripped my chin firmly, turning it to the side. Brushing his scaly thumb over the bruise I gasped slightly as pain shot through it.

"I don't typically like hitting women, but I had to get my point across," he slurred. He released my face quickly as though it was poison to the touch.

"Yeah, well forgive me for calling bullshit on that." He laughed again. He reached up quickly, hooking the top of my shirt and ripping it downward. The fabric shredding, hanging off my shoulder as my bra was partially exposed.

"We have very little time together," he slurred. My heart quickened as he climbed on to the bed in front of me. I pulled on the chains, but they wouldn't give way, and I couldn't move. I tried to make myself small, stuffing myself against the wall as best as I could. I kicked out with my leg, but he grabbed both ankles and spread them, pushing his way between them. I could feel the sick hardness of his dick pressing against my jeans.

"You should have been my daughter." The words hit me like a brick. This was never about my father; this was about my mother.

"Why do you say that?" He laughed again.

"Not to worry, Ellisia, I'm going to take care of you." He grabbed a fistful of my hair and forced his mouth on mine. I tried to pull away, the chains rattling as I tried to fight. I was able to force enough space between our faces so that I slammed my head down on his nose with a sickening crack. He howled as he grabbed his face and stumbled back, blood beginning to stream down, staining his shirt.

"You little bitch!" He lunged at me, throwing a barrage of hits all over my body and face. I covered my head as best as I could, when I felt my hands fall to the mattress, I could still feel the shackles tightly around them. He grabbed the chain and threw me to the ground, kicking me in the center of my body. My screams echoed out as tears fell from my eyes.

"Scream all you want, no one will ever hear you." He snarled. I felt a painful crack in my right side as his boot landed against my ribs. Sending a shrill scream echoing down the empty hallway. I could feel droplets of his blood landing on me as he continued his barrage of kicks. The last one went straight to the side of my head, and I felt the skin split as blood began to run down the side of my face. The force of the blow sent me flying on to my back and I stared up at the ceiling. He leaned over me, wiping the blood from his face, he laughed.

"Someone should have taught you a lesson a long time ago." His smile was wicked as he stood over me. My head throbbing as the strong scent of blood filled my nostrils. I tried to keep my eyes open. I didn't want the sick bastard to touch me. He grabbed my face moving it from side to side. The room began to fade and his face along with it.

"See you in a little bit." His words echoed, following me into the darkness.

When I woke up, I could feel my hands were tied behind my back. Lifting my head, there was a blinding light filtering in. I looked around, confused. This wasn't the room he had been keeping me in. I heard water rushing behind me and turned my head. We were on a dock along the river. A building covering us from the outside world. Like one of those warehouses, you would see in an action film, where the villain is holding the hostage. Just like right now, I was the hostage, for reasons I still didn't understand. All I knew is that it had something to do with my mother. I could see her face clearly in my mind.

"I don't know what I would do without you," her voice echoed in my head. Of all the things that money could have bought her in her life, she said having me was the greatest blessing. She would trade every cent she had just to keep me by her side always. My heart ached for her.

"Your daddy should be here very soon to pick you up, little bird." He snickered, breaking me from my thoughts. I didn't have any more fight in me at this point. We both already knew how this was going to end. He was going to get the money and kill me, possibly my father as well. My breath hitched in my throat as a cry came forward. I would never see Aggie or my mother again, what hurt most is knowing that I would never see Quinn again. Never be able to tell him how I felt. I should have just told him from the get-go who I was and then maybe he wouldn't have been so mad at me.

I wouldn't have left, and this wouldn't be happening.

There was so much I wanted to tell him.

My heart breaking knowing that I would never get the chance.

CHAPTER 42

Quinn

I paced the lobby impatiently, my phone in hand as Aggie sat in one of the lounge chairs, her face in her hands as her legs bounced.

"Why haven't they called? It's nearly three o'clock." My anxiety was kicking up as my mind flashed back to the picture of Lisey on her father's phone. Anger rising inside of me becoming borderline rage.

"Maybe they couldn't get it," Aggie whispered.

"He's David Hammond, there isn't a banker on this planet with the sack to tell him no." Aggie sighed, and I knew there were questions she wanted to ask.

"What?"

"I'm just trying to figure out why after all this time you care so much?"

"Did you not hear me earlier?" I looked at her and her eyes met mine. "I love her."

"Then why did you freak out on her?"

"I was a jackass. I spent my life clawing from the gutters to get where I am today and I was wrong."

"You're damn right you were. Lisey may have grown up with famous parents, but she has worked her ass off getting this far. They didn't hand her a thing. Trust me they tried, and she told them no."

"I didn't know that."

"You never gave her a chance to explain."

"I'm going to apologize for that, for all of it. I want her in my life. Even if I let it all out and she tells me to fuck off, I will spend the rest of my days making it right."

"She won't tell you to fuck off." She stood and walked over, stopping barely a foot away from me.

"You don't think?"

"She loves you, idiot." Her words hit me right in the chest, making my anxiety kick up a thousand notches. I opened my phone; I had waited long enough.

Archie answered on the second ring.

"Have you heard anything?" I asked quickly.

"We just received a location; we are coming to get you now."

"How long?" I heard tires screech in the street outside of the hotel.

"Right now."

"I'll be right out." I ended the call and looked at Aggie. I fished my room key out of my pocket.

"Go upstairs and order whatever you want, just please don't leave." She nodded and gently took the card from me before I darted out the door.

Dark clouds had begun rolling through the city, another day of storms in the forecast. I launched myself into the back seat of Archie's car and he peeled off before I even had time to get my seat belt on.

"Where is she?" I asked as Archie sped down the streets.

"Some boat warehouse along the Water of Leith," Mr. Hammond said.

"Do you know who this guy is?"

"Not a clue."

"Why would he want to hurt Lisey?"

"She's my only daughter, we tried for years to keep her out of the spotlight for fear of something like this happening, but as time has gone on, there have been few that have gotten pictures of all of us together."

"How did she grow up in LA, keeping such a low profile?" Mr. Hammond leaned his head back on the seat, turning to look at me from the front.

"She didn't. She was home schooled and traveled with her mother."

"Is there anyone you could think of that would want to hurt you or her, or even her mother?"

"That list is so long at this point, it would be hard to tell. If I get my hands on the bastard he won't see the break of another dawn. No one touches my little girl and gets away with it." The anger in his voice was palpable, leeching into the energy of the car. I could feel that everyone was amped up.

We stopped where the GPS said to. Before us was a rusty, run-down metal building, the river flowing behind it as heavy raindrops began to pelt it. Mr. Hammond got out of the car, grabbing a suitcase from the trunk. I opened my door.

"Stay with Archie, boy," he instructed. There was no way in hell I was going to stay here and see how this played out. I had to get to Lisey. I nodded and let him go ahead.

As he got closer to the building I began following behind him. My years on the street had taught me how to move quietly through the shadows.

"Quinn!" Archie hissed. I turned to him and shook my head. I had to get in there.

As I got close to the opening, I could hear voices.

"Why? After all this time?" Mr. Hammond's voice echoed.

"You owe me, David."

"For what?"

"Elenor should have been mine. The life you have, the daughter, all of it should have been mine."

"Elenor chose me."

"Because of why?"

"Because I was kinder." I heard a snicker. I peered my head around the corner and saw a tall husk of a man was standing with a gun aimed at Mr. Hammond.

"It was because you were richer, and we both know it."

"Elenor was successful on her own Tobias; she never needed me or my money. She fell in love with my kindness." The man called Tobias spat.

"Spin the story however you like, I don't fucking care, I just want what's mine." He nodded his head towards the briefcase.

"Take it. It's all yours, just give me back, my child." My eyes scanned pass them to Lisey, she was tied to a chair on the edge of the dock. I could see the bruises on her face as well as the dark stains of blood on her clothes. My fists clenched, my nails embedding themselves into my palms, hard enough I could feel blood begin to sweat through my hand. Tobias walked forward the barrel still on Mr. Hammond. He picked it up and backed up towards Lisey. I watched as he half turned as though he was preparing to release her when he picked up his foot and kicked the chair off the dock into the river.

"Ellisia!" Mr. Hammond growled. He charged at Tobias, forcing him to drop the case on the floor, grabbing his arm, he pushed the gun into the air where a single shot fired into the sky before he knocked it free of his grip. I heard the car door slam as Archie came running towards the building, but I didn't wait for him to reach me. I ran in, my feet moving fast underneath me as I made my way to the edge.

"Quinn!" Archie yelled behind me, but it was too late, I dove into the river.

It was dark and I couldn't see anything, she couldn't have gone that far. I kicked up to the surface to grab another gulp of air, I could briefly hear the scuffle on the dock as I dove down again, searching for her. My hands were digging down through the water when I felt hair wrap around my fingers. I propelled myself straight down and my hands found her shoulders. Following them down, I found her hands that were tied behind her back. I quickly fumbled with the ropes, as the last of my air released from my lungs.

As the burning in my lungs began, I felt her hands come free and I grabbed them, wrapping them around my neck as I desperately kicked for the surface.

Breaking through I inhaled a large breath as she drifted against me, starting to go back down. I pulled her head up.

"Lisey." Her lips were pale. There were sirens approaching fast.

"Quinn!" Archie yelled. He was several feet away on a lower dock, leaning over the edge. Supporting Lisey, I swam over, handing her to him. In one quick motion he pulled her from the water, before helping me out. On my knees next to her, I turned her on her back and tilted her head. I put my ear to her chest. I couldn't hear anything. I put my hands into position and started to press down on her chest, lifting her chin and breathing air into her lungs on every thirty count.

"Come on, Lisey," I begged as I continued pumping on her chest. I heard rushed steps approaching me. I tilted her head again and breathed in twice. As I pulled away she heaved upwards, spewing water from her lips. I turned her head to the side quickly so she wouldn't choke.

"Lisey. Lisey, look at me." Tears were in my eyes now. She groaned as she slowly opened her eyes. A hand on my shoulder pulled me away, but I kept my eyes locked on her as she flicked them slightly to me. The paramedics swarmed her, and she coughed before closing her eyes again.

CHAPTER 43

Lisey

I t was a coughing fit that woke me up. Opening my eyes, my vision blurred, I could see faces but couldn't quite make them out.

"Lisey." I recognized the voice right away.

"Daddy?"

"Yes, dove, I'm here." I felt his hand gentle across my forehead, pushing back into my hair. My vision began to center, and I realized I was in a hospital room, Archie, dad, and Quinn sitting around me. My head was pounding, and I inhaled a breath that sent a gasp racing from my lips. I tried to sit up to push back the pain, but it only made it worse. Dad put his hand on my shoulder.

"Take it easy, now."

"Where am I?"

"You're in the hospital and you're safe," dad said. I looked around at each of their faces. The one that surprised me the most was Quinn. I gently reached out my hand to him and Archie cleared his throat.

"We'll give ye some privacy." He stood and dad followed him out into the hallway. Quinn cupped my hand in his, kissing my knuckles hard. I could see in his eyes that he held back tears.

"What are you doing here?" I asked.

"I'm here for you."

"You were so mad at me."

"I was wrong. I'm so sorry, Lisey." I felt tears in my eyes.

"I thought I would never see you again," I said as the tears began to fall freely. He raised his hand and gently brushed them away with his thumb.

"I'm here and you are safe. That man will never be able to hurt you again."

"What happened to him?"

"He was arrested." His face became clear in my mind, and I shuddered. Quinn pulled the blanket up around me, trying to keep me warm.

"You were there," I said as it all came flooding back into my mind. I remembered spitting up the water and I heard someone call my name. Just briefly, it was Quinn's face that etched itself into those last moments before everything went dark.

"I was."

"You pulled me from the water." I could hear the water in the background of my mind, my lungs burning at the memory of not being able to breathe.

"I did."

"Why?" He gently took my chin in his hand and tilted my head up, my eyes locking with his.

"I love you, Ellisia Hammond. I don't care who your parents are. I love you for everything you are and everything you are going to be." More tears streamed down my face as my heart skipped in my chest.

"I love you too, Quinn." He leaned down, our lips colliding together in a hungry kiss that was also gentle. Fireworks were shooting through every nerve in my body. Not so long ago, I never thought I would see him again or be able to tell him how I felt and here we were, safe and alive. He pulled away from me.

"Can you ever forgive me for being the world's largest asshole?" he asked with a slight laugh.

"Only if you can forgive me for being the world's largest jerk. I never should have hired Ayda as your assistant."

"Hey. None of that matters now, all that matters is here right now. You are safe." He touched my cheek gently, sending a tingling throughout my body. For so long, I wanted to push him aside and free myself of him, but now, more than ever, I just wanted him to be with me, in every moment. I was mad at him, but how could I stay mad when he came for me? If he didn't care about me as much as I care about him then he never would have bothered to leave the hotel to go with my dad or Archie.

"It was wrong."

"It was funny and one hundred percent something that I would do." I laughed slightly.

"Good thing I didn't require an assistant," I laughed. He smiled and gently pushed his hand through my hair, twirling a curl with his finger.

"I love you Ellisia Hammond and I will spend every day the rest of my life, making up for the way that I treated you and proving to you how much you mean to me, if you will let me." His words hit me right in the heart. I placed my hand over his as it rested on my cheek and smiled.

"Only if you allow me the same privilege, Mr. Rose." He took my hand in his and pulled it to his lips, running his lips across my knuckles before kissing them hard.

"Every day, from now on."

"Promise?" He leaned in and kissed me softly.

"I promise."

CHAPTER 44

Quinn

"Here we are again, the same old story. We both know we can't pretend; the end will ever change. Tomorrow we will say our last goodbye, so let's live tonight, until the break of morning. Like in our past life." I jumped away from the microphone as the last notes from Marina's and my voice resonated throughout the giant theater. The crowd going crazy.

My blood was pumping so loud that I could feel it in my ears. I looked over at Barry who was wiping sweat of his brow as he prepared his bass for the next song.

I looked off stage. There she was, a smile on her face, as she held Barry and Nina's newborn baby, her own pregnancy peaking just behind the skirt of her dress. She was in conversation; her eyes flicked to mine. Next to her stood Marina's wife, Iliana as Barry's daughters, Kyrie and Ella danced around on the edge. Their laughter drowned out by the cheers of the crowd.

I held my hand out to her. She peered out from the side stage, eyeing the crowd. Looking back at me she shook head no. I stepped up to the mic again.

"I have a special guest with me here tonight. I bet if you give it up, maybe we can get her to join us on stage." The crowd went wild. I looked at her, and she rolled her eyes. I cocked my head with a garish grin. She shook her head again and then handed Nina the baby.

"Lisey?" I said into the mic. She smiled, smoothing out the skirt of her sage green dress, before she walked out on stage. She waved at the crowd as she crossed the floor towards me.

"I told you they would love it," Lisey said in my ear. She pulled away, her smile breaking against my lips as we kissed. I covered the mic with my hand, gently pulling away from her.

"I love you." I said.

"I love you too." I held her hand in mine, gently rubbing my thumb over her knuckles, feeling the diamond ring that now lived on her left ring finger. Holding her hand up, I turned back to the mic.

"Mrs. Rose, published author and soon to be mother." I announced into the mike before bowing my head to her, pulling her hand to my lips, and kissing it gently. There was a loud response from the crowd.

"Such the charmer, Mr. Rose." Her words reached me over the loud crowd. I wrapped my arm around her waist and pulled her close as the beginning chords of the next song started. I could feel her pregnant belly pushing against me and I smiled.

The movie had wrapped eight months ago in Canada. We flew back to Scotland, and we were married in the highlands before we came back home. Here we were four months into my tour, almost a year married and knocking on the doorstep of parenthood, our little man would be here in three short months. She pushed her head into the space between my shoulder and chin. I rested my head against hers. The smell of her hair wafting into my nostrils making everything else fade away.

"Any regrets, Mr. Rose?" She whispered. I lifted my head, my hand finding its way under her chin, lifting her emerald, green eyes to meet mine.

"Never." She smiled at me softly and my heart fluttered. She was everything I ever needed. When I boarded that plane last year, I thought I had everything figured out. She was everything I never knew I wanted.

"I better get back off stage, your audience awaits." Her words brought me back and I found myself still staring into her eyes. Pulling her face gently to mine, I pressed a kiss on her plump pouty lips.

"Today, tomorrow, forever, the only audience I care for is yours and his," I said as I gently pulled away and placed my hand on the side of her belly.

"Ethan Henry Rose."

I smiled, stepping back I knelt down in front of everyone in the venue and kissed her stomach. I couldn't wait to be a dad. I remembered the day she told me she was pregnant. I had been at practice and came home late. We had bought a home just outside of L.A. in the quieter suburb of Redondo Beach, with the help of her parents. She met me at the door and leapt into my arms. I held her tightly as I pressed my lips to hers and then she pulled away, her smile gleaming in the light of the house.

"I'm pregnant."

"What?" Her feet touched the ground again and she pulled a pregnancy test from her back pocket. There it was in bright pink. Two little lines.

The sound of the crowd brought me back from the memory and I smiled, still knelt in front of her. I could feel my son's strong kick against my hand.

"I can't wait to meet you buddy; you have the most beautiful mom; she will read you all of her stories and I will teach you how to play guitar." I looked up at her and smirked. Standing my hand cupped her cheek.

"Go on you," she laughed. I kissed her again, before gently resting my forehead against hers.

"I have the most beautiful wife." Her cheeks flushed in the cutest way.

"You have to get back. I love you." She lifted her lips to mine and kissed me again as my fingers tangled in her soft brown curls. She pulled away and my finger trailed down her cheek, holding her gaze just a little bit longer.

"I love you too, Ellisia Rose."

"Forever?" I smiled at her question. There was time when I wanted nothing more than to get away from her. I spent my life trying to forge a home for myself. She had become my home. Lisey and our son were all the home I would ever need.

"No matter the weight the world throws at us, we will shoulder it together, pound for pound. Until my last breath."

Acknowledgements

A huge thank you to my readers and supporters who have been following along, whether it's with this new story or the Hunted series. Without you guys this dream of mine wouldn't be real

Thank you my amazing publishing team at Golden Light Publishing House. Yvonne Hamilton and B Wills, for believing in me and keeping me in check. I know I can get crazy at times with 4 am messages about release dates and forgetting to save edits before formatting. (Sorry. Love you!) You ladies keep me grounded and I am forever grateful to be on this wonderful journey with you at Golden Light.

Thank you to my dear friend Racheal Shantel, who took my hand and showed me the way. I am forever grateful that after all of our time apart that we have reunited, forging a sisterhood on this journey together. Supporting each other one novel at a time. Love you Big!

Thank you to the Chaos Crew, Rebecca Kulp, M.A. Worrell, Stephanie B, ya'll keep me smiling and propel me forward. Thank you for sticking by me and keeping me smiling through it all, even though I make you mad with all of my twists and turns. You ladies have no idea how much I value our friendship.

Thank you to Dwayne, who is without a doubt the greatest blessing in my life. From the first day I said I wanted to go back to writing, you stood by my side and supported me. I never imagined that this is where getting back to what I loved would go, but I'm so blessed to have you by my side for all of it. Every rewrite, every edit, the long nights, the meetings. Your patience, love and devotion don't go unnoticed. I love you so much.

Much Love,

S Lynn C

ABOUT THE
AUTHOR

S Lynn C

S Lynn C is 34 years old, and lives in Ohio. An avid animal lover, with the dream of writing since she was 13.

She is the Author of Hunted: The Isabel Twain Story and is debuting her first dark romance.

S Lynn C signed with Golden Light Publishing House in 2025.

ALSO BY

S Lynn C

Hunted: The Isabel Twain Story

Abducted – Book 1

Into the Storm - Book 2

Book 3 - 2026

More Coming Soon...